Virtu...

Russell Stannard was formerly Professor of Physics
at the Open University at Milton Keynes. He has
travelled widely in Europe and the USA, research-
ing high-energy nuclear physics. He has received
the Templeton UK project award and has spent a
year in America as a visiting fellow at the Center of
Theological Theory, Princeton. He was recently
awarded an OBE for services to physics and the
popularisation of science.

Married with four children of his own and three
stepchildren, he vividly remembers the excitement
of discovering Einstein's theories for the first time
and he is now dedicated to passing this inspiration
on to new generations. *The Time and Space of Uncle
Albert* was shortlisted for both the Science Award
and the Whitbread Award, and his books have
been translated into seventeen different languages.

by the same author

THE TIME AND SPACE OF UNCLE ALBERT
BLACK HOLES AND UNCLE ALBERT
UNCLE ALBERT AND THE QUANTUM QUEST
ASK UNCLE ALBERT: 100½ TRICKY SCIENCE QUESTIONS ANSWERED
THE WORLD OF 1001 MYSTERIES
DR DYER'S ACADEMY
HERE I AM!

RUSSELL STANNARD

Virtutopia

faber and faber

First published in 2003
by Faber and Faber Limited
3 Queen Square London WC1N 3AU

Typeset by Faber and Faber
Printed in England by Mackays of Chatham plc, Chatham, Kent

A CIP record for this book
is available from the British Library

ISBN 0–571–21700–1

2 4 6 8 10 9 7 5 3 1

Virtutopia

One

A Plan

'We're lost,' announced Lucie, glaring in frustration at the trees pressing in on them from every side.

'No, we're not,' replied Scott over his shoulder, continuing his trudge down the path.

'I tell you we are,' she insisted. 'We've come in a circle.'

Her brother stopped and looked back at her. 'What do you mean?'

'I recognise the tree.'

'You recognise the *tree*!' replied Scott. 'We're in the middle of a forest; we've been surrounded by trees for the past hour; and now you say you *recognise* a tree. They all look the same, stupid.'

'Not that one,' Lucie replied quietly, gazing up at the split and blackened branches of a pine that had clearly been struck by lightning at some time in the past.

'Oh,' murmured Scott. 'I see what you mean.'

'This is where we had our sandwiches, remember?' she continued, sitting down on the trunk of a fallen tree.

Scott nodded miserably, and joined her.

Tall, dark-haired Lucie Harris was the elder by a couple of years. Scott was a bit of a scruff, though, to tell the truth, both of them were pretty hot and dirty after what they had already been through. Up to now he had confidently led the way, slashing at the bramble bushes on either side so that they would not scratch his sister's legs. But now he felt defeated. 'I don't get it. How did that happen?' he complained.

'Oh, it's the usual problem with you. You never *think*,' scolded his sister. 'What we needed was a plan – some system to make sure we didn't just keep going round in a circle.'

'But I did have a plan,' Scott protested. 'A good plan.'

'Oh, yes,' replied Lucie sceptically. 'And what, may I ask, was your great plan? You come to a fork in the path – and goodness knows we've seen enough of those – a fork in the path, so what do you do? Which fork do you take?'

'Simple. I took the fork that looked most *trodden down*. That's where most people go. OK? Satisfied?'

Lucie fell silent for a little while, before eventually murmuring, 'Sorry. I'm sorry, Scott. It was a good plan. The only trouble with it is that most people seem to have got it wrong; they must all be going in circles.'

'Got any better idea? We've got to get out of this place quick,' said Scott anxiously. 'It's getting dark. We shall soon not be able to see where we are going. In any case,' he added with a puzzled frown, 'I've been wondering: how did we get here in the first place? What are we doing in a forest at all?'

'That's something *I've* been wondering about. I don't remember. But anyway, that's neither here nor there. You're right: we need to get out quick. We need some other plan. We need to be able to take our bearings. A compass, for example.'

'Oh, silly me,' said Scott sarcastically, as he rummaged in his jacket pockets, 'I seem to have come without mine.'

Ignoring him she continued. 'Pity about the clouds. Could have taken a direction from the sun.'

'I know. How about moss?' said Scott brightening up.

'Moss?'

'Yes – you know. Moss grows on the north side of the tree trunk – the side that doesn't get the sun so much – so it's colder and damper. That would tell us which way was north – it would be a sort of compass.'

'Good thinking,' said Lucie approvingly.

Unfortunately their hopes were rapidly dashed. An inspection of the trees showed that the trunks were covered by moss on all sides.

'I guess it's always so dark and gloomy here the sunlight never gets through,' declared Lucie. Suddenly she jumped. 'What was that?' she hissed.

'What was what?' asked her brother.

'Over there. Something moved.'

'Over where?'

'There,' she said, pointing. 'I could swear I saw something move.'

'I can't see anything. Are you sure?'

She nodded. 'Yes. Well . . . It's hard to tell with the light going.'

'Probably just some animal – coming out to hunt at night.'

'Hunt?' asked Lucie fearfully. 'Hunt for what?'

Scott shrugged. 'No, no, it's probably nothing. A trick of the light. Forget it. What about our plan? Got any more ideas?'

Lucie thought for a moment, then her eyes lit up. 'Yes, that would do it,' she announced. 'The slope. We can use the slope. See what I mean? There is a slope – well . . . sort of; there are a few ups and downs, but generally it's going down in that direction,' she indicated. 'If we always take the fork that takes us *down*, then we can't keep coming back to the same spot.'

'Hey, that's right. Or, of course, we might always take the one going up. Yes, how about that? If we get to the top of this hill we might come out of the forest at some point, then we'll be high up and can get a good view and see where we are.'

'Ye . . . es,' said Lucie uncertainly. 'But what if it's trees all the way up to the top? Then we would be no better off. No, I reckon it would be better to keep going down. That way we might eventually find a road. Roads go round the bottom of hills, not over the top of them.'

'Fair enough,' agreed Scott. 'I'm getting tired anyway, and it'll be easier going down.'

No sooner had they set out than Lucie let out a piercing scream. Trembling, she pointed to something lying across the path ahead of them. 'A snake,' she exclaimed. 'Can you see it?'

It certainly looked like a snake. Scott, armed with his trusty stick ventured forward and prodded it. He bent down and suddenly grasped it. Immediately, it jumped and caught him in the throat. 'Urgh!' he cried, falling to the ground. Lucie was horrified as she looked on helplessly. Scott lay lifeless on the path. Cautiously she approached the prone figure. On getting close, however, she noticed his body was not at all lifeless; on the contrary, Scott was shaking with silent laughter.

'Scott!' she said sternly.

The boy rolled over onto his back. 'It's OK, little sister. I have saved you. I have killed the wicked monster,' he said, holding up the fallen branch. With that, Lucie went into a sobbing rage as she pummelled him with her fists. 'Don't you ever, ever do that to me again,' she demanded. 'That was a horrible thing to do. You should be ashamed of yourself.'

Eventually she calmed down, and they continued their journey, Scott leading the way, following their new strategy of always taking the fork leading downwards. From time to time, he would stamp on anything suspicious in their path – 'just in case', as he put it. Every now and again they heard strange sounds and rustling in the undergrowth. Branches brushed their faces unexpectedly as it became increasingly difficult to see them in the gathering gloom.

After proceeding in this manner for half an hour, Lucie ventured, 'The trees are beginning to thin out.'

'No, they're not,' replied her brother.

They carried on.

'Yes, they are,' said Lucie firmly.

'Hmm. I think you might actually be right,' agreed Scott.

And she was. Quite suddenly they were out of the forest. The trees came to an abrupt halt where the ground became rocky. They looked about them. No road in sight. Instead, beyond the rocks they could see a beach. They were at the edge of a sea.

'Which sea – or lake – would that be, I wonder?' murmured Lucie. Neither of them knew.

Far off to their right, in the direction where the beach stretched, the clouds had begun to disperse in that part of the sky. The sun, which was already below the horizon, was leaving a red afterglow. The thin crescent of the moon peeped through a gap in the clouds; it would soon be following the sun.

'It won't be long before it's dark,' said Lucie. 'And with the moon about to set as well as the sun, it'll be pitch black tonight. We won't be able to see a thing. We'll have to wait for morning. Then we'll be able to walk along the beach. We're bound to come to a town or something eventually.'

'So, what do you reckon?' asked Scott. 'We ought to get a bit of shut-eye.'

'I guess so,' his sister replied. 'But I'm not sleeping *here*,' she added with a shiver, glancing back at the grim and threatening forest. 'There's no accounting for what might come out of there in the middle of the night. We'd better get down onto the beach as far away from the forest as we can.'

It was only a short clamber. Scott at one point slipped on a piece of seaweed and grazed his ankle on a rock but it was nothing serious. Soon they stepped onto smooth dry sand. The tide was far out, but they could rinse off some of the dirt in a rock pool. Lucie made sure Scott cleaned his graze as best he could.

9

'Got any more food on you?' she asked when they had finished.

Scott searched his pockets and pulled out a battered-looking bar of chocolate.

'You break it and I'll choose,' said his sister.

'No. *You* break it and I'll choose. It's my chocolate, so I get to choose,' insisted Scott.

'Suit yourself,' she said, taking the bar and breaking it carefully to make the halves as equal as possible. She offered them to Scott, who studied them long and hard.

'Oh, for goodness' sake get on with it,' said Lucie impatiently. 'I'm tired. They are exactly the same.'

As they munched away, her brow furrowed. 'What is that glow over there?' she asked.

Although to the extreme west the clouds were breaking up, they were still thick across the rest of the sky. What Lucie had noticed was that the clouds to the east, low down on the horizon, were glowing.

'Street lights,' declared Scott. 'Stray light from street lamps shining up onto the clouds. There must be a big town over there. Which is good. That tells us which direction we should be heading tomorrow – back to civilisation. Perhaps then we'll be able to find out where we are – and how we come to be here.'

Lucie gently shook her head. 'No,' she said thoughtfully. 'That's not it. Street lights are yellow. That light is white.'

'*Some* street lights are white. They're not all yellow.'

'In any case, it is not the underside of the clouds that are lit. The light is shining *through* them. You can tell.'

'It must be the moon coming up,' said Scott with a yawn, beginning to settle down for the night on the soft sand.

'No it can't be that. The moon is over there,' she said, pointing to the opposite horizon. 'At least it *was* a minute ago. No, it's odd. I'd have thought *that* part of the sky – to the east – should be the darkest. But it's not.'

Scott lost interest. He was too busy making up a pile of sand for a pillow. Having done that to his satisfaction, he stretched out and was asleep in no time. Lucie was left sitting there, hunched up, hands clasped round her knees, puzzling over the strange light in the east. It seemed to her that, if anything, it was getting brighter. But it was hard to tell. Perhaps her eyes were just getting used to the dark.

Two

The Promise

The scene: the imposing headquarters of VirtuCorp – one of the leading multi-national corporations. It was the day of an eagerly awaited press conference. Reporters from all over the world had come. For weeks beforehand, speculation had run riot as to what kind of announcement was to be made. But no one knew for certain; it had been a closely guarded secret. Now all was to be revealed.

But not just yet. Lord Harsk, the Chief Executive Officer, had a keen sense of the dramatic. He was determined to build up the tension even further before he took the stage. So it was that, much to the irritation of some of those assembled, they all had first to sit through a talk about the company's past achievements. This was delivered by the Senior Scientist, Dr Theodore Birkin – a thin, gangling figure, with wispy grey hair sticking out in all directions. He wore baggy trousers and an ill-fitting, shabby sports coat. This was draped over him as though it had been carelessly flung onto a clothes hanger. He looked everyone's idea of the mad scientist – apart from his eyes; these were kindly and gentle, not the staring, manic sort of eyes one might expect.

He began by explaining how VirtuCorp, when it was originally set up, was much like the other companies in the video games market. Like certain of its rivals, it went on to develop headsets, so giving the optical illusion that one was immersed in some kind of virtual reality. Over time, the scenes being viewed became more and more realistic. By pressing buttons on a console, one could 'explore' this virtual environment – as though one were walking through it, turning corners, etc. But at this stage, it was purely an optical phenomenon.

'Then came VirtuCorp's big breakthrough,' continued Dr Birkin. 'The cybersuit. As you will all know, this gave sensory perceptions over the entire body that were indistinguishable from the real thing. This gave rise to unprecedented realism – whether in video games, flight simulators, or whatever. From now on, one not only *saw* a virtual environment, one fully *experienced* it. The cybersuit produced a personal climate for oneself in terms of temperature and humidity. Sensors embedded throughout the suit could exert pressures on any part of the body. And electrodes in the headset fed signals directly into the brain, so stimulating mental sensations, and enhancing the full experience.

'Then finally, as we announced last year, came IPVR – Inter Personal Virtual Reality. Two people, both wearing cybersuits, are linked to each other through the Internet. This way I would be able to interact with you,' said Birkin picking on one of the audience, 'as though we were in the same room – even though in reality we might be on opposite sides of the world. If you decide to take a punch at me (meaning you take a swing at the *image* of me which you see in front of you), then your fist feels a jolt as it connects with my supposed body. In actuality, of course, it is the part of the suit covering your fist that delivers that jolt to you. But what you *feel* is exactly the same as hitting a real body. Meanwhile, I – wherever I might be located – simultaneously feel a prod in the chest or the chin; this is delivered by the relevant part of *my* cybersuit. Or suppose I take a fancy to some good-looking woman,' he said mischievously gazing round the room before fixing his attention on a female reporter in the second row. 'I take the image of her in my arms and make to kiss her, and for me it will feel exactly as though I was hugging and kissing her – that much being ensured by my cybersuit. She at the same time – through the Internet connection – will be made to feel as though she has been taken into my arms and I am kissing her. That is what *her* cybersuit is doing to her.'

'In your dreams, Dr Birkin. In your dreams,' the reporter replied, causing a loud outburst of laughter.

'Of course,' replied Dr Birkin with a twinkle in his eye, 'all of this could only happen with the lady's co-operation. As far as taking responsibility for one's actions is concerned, IPVR is no different from real life. It will not have escaped your attention, these virtual interactions have become so real that the law courts have now ruled that whatever you do to someone else through IPVR counts in law as though it happened directly. In the case of a mugging, say, carried out through the medium of IPVR, the criminal can no longer claim that he was not at the scene of the crime. You might recall the case of Johnson vs. Bruckheimer. The victim, Johnson was in London, while Bruckheimer was in New York at the time of the attack. But that was held to be no defence because the two were at the time linked through IPVR.'

'What about the Hanson case?' interjected a reporter. 'Do you agree with the verdict that he was guilty of murder?'

'Certainly,' Birkin replied. 'He knew he was connected up to IPVR; he knew what it was capable of doing; he deliberately took up the gun . . .'

'But it was only a *virtual* gun. That's my point. It wasn't *real*.'

'Makes no difference,' the scientist declared firmly. 'If you are connected by IPVR, the virtual gun is *just as dangerous* as the real thing. The injury delivered to the victim, as a result of the culprit's action, is just as lethal as if it were delivered by a real bullet. So the accused was guilty – guilty of murder. These changes in the law were needed.'

'So how does that make *you* feel?' asked a TV reporter getting up from the front row and thrusting his microphone forward towards the speaker.

'How does it make *me* feel?' asked Birkin. 'Sorry, I don't see what you're getting at.'

'Well, the victim would not have been killed if your cybersuit had not lethally penetrated the body of the victim. The cybersuit – which was designed and manufactured by VirtuCorp – caused a wound indistinguishable from that of a *bullet*, for God's sake. Don't you think that was – to put it mildly – irresponsible of you?'

This question brought murmurs of approval from those who apparently felt the same. But these were cut short as Lord Harsk himself abruptly sprang to his feet. He confronted the reporter.

'Look, man, what kind of business do you think we're in here?' he barked. 'This is not a *toy* factory. We aren't in the business of making electronic *games* – not any more. This is a virtual reality.' With that, Harsk poked the reporter in the chest and added, 'And the emphasis is on *reality*.' Smiling expansively at the audience he continued. 'And as a reality, it has to be taken seriously; it has to be handled responsibly – like any other reality. Cybersuits can kill – if misused – just like a car, or a knife, or almost anything else. If someone misuses IPVR, you can hardly blame us for it – any more than a car manufacturer is to blame for a drunk-driving accident.'

Lord Harsk made an imposing figure. He was a large man in every sense. With gingery-blond hair going grey at the temples, he had a big mouth, closely set dark brown eyes which looked right through you, a face set into a perpetual scowl, a coarse overbearing manner, and a booming voice which penetrated doors and echoed down corridors. In contrast to the shambling figure of his Senior Scientist, he was immaculately dressed in an expensive dark suit with a red rose in his button-hole.

A hand was tentatively raised.

'Have you any comments to make, sir, on the Church's ruling last week that it was adultery to have sex with other people through IPVR?'

'I personally do not avail myself of that experience – at least, not too often,' Harsk replied with a leer. 'But I understand from those who do make a habit of that sort of thing that it is just as good as the old-fashioned way of doing it. Not only that, but it can be more convenient doing it without either of you having to leave your own homes. So yes, I reckon it's adultery – and grounds for divorce. The sheer reality of IPVR is now universally recognised, and that stands as a tribute to the quality of the product we produce here.'

'Excuse me, Lord Harsk,' intervened a well-known and distinguished television newsman. 'But all we have been told so far this morning is nothing new. The cybersuit has been around for a number of years now. I am sure you have not brought us together just to tell us what we already know. Forgive me, but is it too much to ask if we could get to the point as to why we are here? Some of us have deadlines to meet . . .' he said, looking at his watch.

'Yes, yes, of course,' Lord Harsk beamed. 'Dr Birkin was just filling in the background for you.' He turned to the scientist and rudely waved him aside. 'That'll be all, Birkin; I'll take over from here.'

He gazed round the room, clearly relishing every moment.

'The aim so far has been to replicate, as realistically as we can, our normal world. We make interacting with others through IPVR as close as possible to the real thing. When you are in that virtual reality, it is quite impossible to tell that it is fake. But now we have developed a master programme that will allow us to *alter* the environment in which the IPVR interactions take place. We can replicate what it would be like to live in worlds different from ours.'

'Different in what way?' asked the same reporter. 'Create new sceneries – landscapes – that sort of thing?'

'That yes, but also worlds where . . .' Harsk paused for effect – 'worlds where the laws of nature are different.'

Just then there was a commotion as a TV cameraman unbalanced and fell off the chair upon which he had been precariously perched. He picked himself up and apologised profusely.

'A world where gravity wasn't so strong, perhaps?' called out a voice. Lord Harsk joined in the laughter, bellowing out, 'And why not? No more grazed knees. Good idea!'

Once order was restored, he continued. 'Seriously though, we are now in the position of developing alternative virtual worlds. And this is why we have called you here today.'

All attention was riveted on the Chief Executive as he declared, 'I am proud to announce that VirtuCorp is about to produce the very best of all possible worlds. In the near future, we shall be able to leave this messy world with its many problems – earthquakes; plane crashes; car pile-ups; rising crime rates; child abuse; wars; disease; lack of justice – and instead enter into, and indeed, permanently *live* in an entirely new world. We are about to create a world where all will be well – the *perfect* world. It will be the kind of world God *ought* to have created – if he had done his job properly,' he sniggered. 'So, it gives me great pleasure to unveil VirtuCorp's latest project. The production of a virtual reality that is the world of our dreams – indeed, a utopia. We call it . . .'

He paused. Then with a flourish, he pulled a cord hanging by his side. Immediately the silken cloth on the wall behind him, displaying the name and emblem of the company, fell to the ground. In its place was revealed the name:

VIRTUTOPIA

19

A buzz of excitement swept round the packed room. The place was lit up with scores of flash bulbs.

When the excitement had subsided a little, Lord Harsk went on to forecast that, with the ever-reducing working week and with earlier retirement, people would in times to come spend the vast majority of their lives in this virtual world – interacting with their families and others through IPVR.

'Sir,' interrupted a woman reporter, 'this sounds . . . well, it sounds wonderful. Nothing short of perfection indeed. But I can't help wondering whether it is too good to be true.'

'Oh and why is that, my dear?' purred Lord Harsk condescendingly.

She bristled at his manner, but continued. 'What I don't understand is why – if God got it wrong, as you put it – why is it you think you'll be able to do any better?'

Harsk pursed his lips and shrugged. 'How should I know why he screwed up? Perhaps he's *not* as powerful as he is cracked up to be – things got out of control. Or perhaps he's not as *good* as people say he is – he has a nasty streak. Perhaps he doesn't exist *at all*. How should I know? All I do know is that none of this is a problem for us. VirtuCorp most definitely *exists*,' he said with a grand gesture. 'And VirtuCorp has *complete control* over the virtual realities it creates.'

'That's as may be,' the woman replied. 'But what you don't have is complete control over the people taking part in IPVR. They – as far as I understand you – they are to be normal people brought up in *this* world – what you choose to call this *messy* world. So won't these less-than-perfect people mess up your precious Virtutopia as soon as they get into it – assuming you haven't messed it up yourself already?'

Harsk gave her a superior smile. 'But, my dear, you are mistaken – entirely mistaken. We *do* have complete control. No one will be able to mess up our Virtutopia because,' he stated slowly and menacingly, 'because we shall not *permit* it.'

Turning to the audience at large, he explained. 'You see, people can enter Virtutopia only by means of their cybersuits – their *programmable* cybersuits,' he added with emphasis. 'We shall build into the system a security-checking procedure that will allow only certain forms of behaviour by the suits – *acceptable* forms of behaviour.'

'But what about computer viruses being injected by wilful individuals? Have you thought of that?' asked another reporter.

Harsk brushed him aside. 'Of course we've thought of it. It is not a problem. We have developed foolproof anti-virus programs. Next question.'

'Surely a perfect world can only be produced by someone who is himself perfect,' suggested another. 'I take it you are not claiming to be perfect yourself. So how are you going to ensure that your *own* faults and weaknesses don't get into this Virtutopia of yours?'

Harsk gave the questioner a sly, knowing look. 'No one in their right mind would accuse *me* of being perfect. I did not get where I am by being *good*. The "Virtu" part of our name does not point to any particular virtue in me,' he smirked. 'No, I am not creating Virtutopia out of any benign motive; I have a more powerful one than that: commercial gain. What will sell this virtual reality concept is that it will be perfect. That's the *promise*. That's what people will be buying – an escape from all their troubles. If it is *not* perfect – if it does not deliver the goods promised – it will not *sell*. VirtuCorp has no alternative but to make this world perfect – in order to make a *profit* for its shareholders. *That* is the guarantee of success.'

'What about unforeseen circumstances?' asked the woman who had spoken up before. 'How can you be sure things will work out the way you think they will?'

'Again, that is not a problem. We have programs that will run through all possible scenarios. That's what we shall be doing between now and the launch date.'

'*When* is the launch date?'

'Currently we are in the design stage. We are identifying what makes for the perfect world – a world exactly tailored to meet the wishes and needs of the public. When that is successfully completed – which shouldn't take long – we shall then install the system and be ready for launch February next year.'

'How much is it going to cost?' asked the last questioner.

The Financial Director passed a sheet of paper to Lord Harsk, pointing to something written on it.

'Ah yes . . . Yes, the cost of the cybersuit will be £9,995. But of course, that's just the recommended retail price; you are advised to shop around,' Harsk said with a laugh. 'So, as you see, it is no more than the cost of a small car. And we expect that price to come down when we go into mass production. And as for the annual fee for unlimited access to IPVR via the Internet . . . Yes . . . that looks as though it will be somewhere in the region of £500 per year – give or take. So, all in all, I think you'll agree that's one hell of a deal. After all, how much time do you spend in a car each day? Compare that to the usage you will get out of this. Believe me, Virtutopia is going to be so wonderful, people will in future be spending most of their life in a cybersuit. After all, why live in this messy world when you can equally easily live in the utopian world of your dreams – in Virtutopia?'

Three

Moonshine

'Wake up; wake up!' urged Lucie as she shook Scott's shoulder.

'What? Morning already?' murmured her brother, yawning. He slowly roused himself, shielding his eyes from the bright light.

'Look!' she said, staring up at the sky. 'Look at that!'

He blinked as his gaze followed hers. 'What the . . .?' He gaped in open-mouthed astonishment. 'What . . .? What is it? A space ship – a flying saucer?' he breathed.

The clouds had by now almost completely dispersed, revealing a starry sky. Right above them there floated a vast, disk-shaped object. It had a diameter about ten times that of the moon, and shone with a brilliant silvery-white light. It was not moving – as far as they could tell. It just seemed to hang there.

'No, I don't think it's a space ship,' said Lucie. 'Space ships don't look like that. It has craters on it. And mountains. See?' She pointed out a range of mountains running down the right-hand side.

'Is it the moon?' asked Scott.

'I don't think so. It's too big for that.'

'But it might be the moon. It might be falling out of the sky and getting closer,' suggested Scott anxiously. 'That would make it look bigger.'

'Ye-es . . . But it hasn't been getting any larger; I've been watching it ever since it came out from behind the clouds. Besides, the moon set ages ago over there,' she nodded in the direction where they had earlier seen it go down.

They stared in wonder at the spectacle, pointing out to each other its various features: lofty mountains, deep valleys, craters, and craters within other craters. They became so engrossed, they failed to recognise the first signs of danger: the distant sound of waves. If they did hear them, they thought nothing of it. What else would one expect to hear on a beach? But then the noise became louder and more intense. A storm brewing, perhaps? That was unlikely given that there were hardly any clouds now. Then the rhythmic sound of waves gradually transformed into a different sound: the roar of rushing water – a torrent. They peered out to sea. They could see nothing but flat sandy beach. But then, suddenly, to their horror, they caught sight of it: a great tidal wave surging towards them out of the gloom. The foaming top was brilliantly lit by the light from above. It towered higher than a three-storey house.

The terrified children turned and fled for their lives. As fast as they could, they scrambled over the rocks, up and up towards the forest. All thoughts about his grazed ankle forgotten, Scott manfully tried to keep up with Lucie. But she was racing ahead with her long legs. 'Hurry! Hurry!' she called out to him.

Too late. With a thunderous roar, the wave crashed against the rocks, sending spray hurtling upwards. The violence of the impact sent a shudder through the rock face – a shudder with the force of an earthquake. Scott lost his footing and fell backwards into the seething, heaving waters.

'*Scott*!' screamed Lucie, looking back in terror over her shoulder. 'Scott! Where are you?' Frantically she looked about her. A confusion of glistening rocks, churning water, and bright foam. But no Scott.

Four

The Return

'Scott, Scott, it's OK. You're back. It's all over.' It was Theodore Birkin. He whipped off Scott's headset. He then hurried over to the other platform calling out, 'It's all right, Lucie. It's finished. You're safe. Both of you.' He removed Lucie's.

She looked about her wildly, 'Scott, Scott! Where . . .?' Catching sight of him across the laboratory, she let out a sigh of relief.

Scott, looking bewildered, stepped unsteadily off his platform. He felt himself all over to make sure he really was still alive after his ordeal. Then his face broke into a broad grin. 'Wow! That was *cool*!' he declared. 'Unbelievable!'

Lucie rushed over to him and gave him a warm hug.

'Wasn't that great?' he cried.

'Ye-es,' she replied, a little uncertainly. 'That was quite an experience.'

'But it felt real, right?' Scott insisted. 'You couldn't tell it was fake at all.'

'It certainly fooled me,' she agreed.

Dr Birkin smiled. 'Better get your suits off. Do it carefully. They're a bit tight.' He helped them get unzipped.

Peeling his off, Scott looked puzzled. He felt inside the suit. 'I don't understand.'

'Don't understand what?' asked Birkin.

'How come it's dry? It ought to be soaking wet, but it isn't. It's bone dry. And . . .' He put his finger on his tongue. 'The saltiness. It's gone. I had a mouthful of water just now. It tasted horrible. But it's gone. I can't taste anything now. Have I swallowed it, or what?'

Birkin smiled and explained there had been no water – none at all. It had all been virtual. The feeling of wetness had largely been the result of temperature changes in the suit; the salty taste had been produced by the electrodes. 'These,' he said, pointing to the tiny metal plates carefully positioned over the inside of the headset. 'These send electrical signals to the various parts of your brain. Instead of the signals arriving in the normal way – from the taste buds in your mouth, say – we put exactly the same signals into the relevant part of your brain directly – through your skull – using these.'

'So, are you saying the pushes, and pulls, and changes of temperature we felt were real – produced by the suit – but everything else we experienced was phoney, all in the mind? Is that it?' asked Scott.

'Exactly,' agreed Birkin. 'One or the other, or sometimes a mixture of both. It all depends on what sensation we are trying to create. That feeling of wetness was actually a mixture – a change of temperature produced by the suit, supplemented by a mild electrical stimulation.'

Scott frowned. 'So while we were in that virtual reality – in the forest and down on the beach, we – I mean, the *real* us – we were here on the platforms. We were here all the time; we never actually left this room?'

'That's right. You were here all the time.'

'And where were you?'

'Next door. Come, I'll show you.' He led them out of the lab, through an interconnecting door, and into the next room – the control room.

One wall was completely covered from floor to ceiling with monitor screens. The other three sides of the room housed stacks of electronics and computer cabinets. Dr Birkin went over and sat at the console in the middle of the room, facing the screens. 'From here I can keep tabs on everything going on.'

The children noted with interest that some of the screens were showing the beach and others were trained on different parts of the forest.

'That's where we sat down and had our sandwiches,' said Scott pointing excitedly to a screen showing the fallen log.

'And the tree I *recognised*,' added Lucie knowingly, indicating the tree in the background that had been struck by lightning.

'So, now you've tried it, what do you think?' asked the scientist.

'Great,' enthused Scott. 'I've heard of this sort of thing before, of course. I've read about it. But I've never had a chance to try it out for myself. It's so incredibly *real*.'

'Yes, it's quite something,' agreed his sister. 'And did you do all this yourself, Dr Birkin?'

'Call me Theo,' the scientist replied. 'If we are going to be working together I think we need to be on first-name terms, yes?'

'All right . . . *Theo*.' Lucie smiled shyly.

'Yes, it was my design. Obviously I get a lot of help – technical support – that kind of thing. But this type of virtual reality, and IPVR in general, you could say it was my brainchild. So,' he continued, leaning forward earnestly and looking back and forth between the two of them, 'are you game to help me out with the project?'

'You bet!' exclaimed Scott, eyes shining.

'Well . . .' said Lucie more cautiously. 'Could you tell us a bit more about it? What *exactly* do you want us to do?'

Theo shrugged. 'What more do you want to know? It's as I told you when we had that meeting with your parents. We aim to develop this perfect virtual world – Virtutopia. But before we go ahead and build it, we need to check out what the public wants from it – what kind of world they would like. At least, that's what *I* think. The boss, Lord Harsk, he doesn't see it as a problem. He reckons we already know what everyone wants. But I'm not so sure we do. In my view, we ought to sound out opinions – particularly the opinions of the younger generation. After all, you children are what the future is all about. And when it comes to anything to do with computers and new developments, children, not adults, are the ones who master them quickest and who feel most at home with them. So that's why I want you to spend your summer holiday trying out different types of Virtutopia for me. See which you prefer – and whether there are any snags associated with them – drawbacks we did not anticipate. We call it "developmental testing".'

'And we get paid for this, right?' Scott intervened eagerly.

'That's the idea, yes. You'll get paid for your trouble. Not a great deal.'

'How much?'

'I still have to settle that with your parents.' Theo smiled. 'So. What do you think? Are you in on this with me?'

Scott looked at Lucie. 'You know what I think,' he said.

'I'm not so sure,' replied his sister doubtfully.

'Oh come on!' declared Scott in exasperation. 'Honestly!' He turned to Theo. 'Typical. That's *girls* for you!'

Lucie flushed with anger. 'All right. I'm game too,' she announced.

'Excellent!' exclaimed Theo. 'After all, what have you got to lose?'

'Our lives!' muttered Lucie. 'If that last episode was anything to go by. In any case,' she added as an afterthought, 'what *was* that moon business all about?'

'Yes. I've been wondering about that. Does Virtutopia have an extra moon or something?' asked Scott.

'No, no. That virtual reality you visited had nothing to do with Virtutopia. That was just a trial run to give you the feel for what living in a virtual reality is like – just helping you to get used to the system. No, we haven't begun to think of how we want to vary things to change our sort of world into something better – a Virtutopia.'

'But *our* world hasn't got a second moon like that,' protested Lucie.

'Er . . . no. No, it hasn't,' agreed Theo. 'That virtual reality you just visited wasn't *exactly* like our world. I suppose the trouble is when you've spent as long as I have playing around with exact copies of this world, you can't help getting a bit bored with them. So, I thought I'd liven things up a bit for you by having an extra moon – one that was sufficiently close for you to be able to make out the craters without the help of binoculars or a telescope. After all, in our type of universe – with its particular laws of nature – there was nothing to stop Earth having a second moon – one that was closer than the other one. Such things are just a matter of chance. So it was only stretching things a little bit. The trouble was, at the time I programmed the new moon into the system, I didn't realise you were going to get so close to the sea edge.'

'And that rush of water. What was that all about? Do I take it that had something to do with the extra moon? A tide, or something?' asked Lucie.

'Yes. That was the tide coming in. It was that much higher and more spectacular because of the closeness of the moon.'

Lucie looked at the scientist searchingly. 'Tell me: when Scott fell into the water, could he have died? It was only fake water; we know that now. So, do I take it he wasn't in any *real* danger? It was just to scare us?'

Theo looked uncomfortable. He shifted in his seat, then murmured apologetically, 'Yes, there *was* a possibility of him being killed – the danger was real. Mind you,' he added hastily, gesturing to the monitor screens opposite, 'I was monitoring your movements all the time.'

'Oh!' said Scott angrily. 'You were watching us all the time. You could see the tide coming in; you could see me scrambling over the rocks to get away. But you just sat back and let it happen. If you knew all about it, why didn't you do something – rescue us?'

'But I did,' protested the scientist. 'I did rescue you. I got you back here.'

'*Eventually*,' exploded Scott. 'But not until I had half drowned. Why didn't you get us out earlier?'

'I couldn't,' was the reply. 'When I return you to this world, by double clicking this "release" icon,' he said indicating the icons on the screen – one labelled RELEASE SCOTT and the other RELEASE LUCIE – you suddenly disappear out of the virtual-reality world. We can't do that at *any* time – just to suit ourselves. It would be very confusing for someone else in that world to have people suddenly vanishing in front of their eyes; it would destroy the illusion that they were in a real world. So built into the program is the requirement that I cannot get you back if you are in someone else's presence – if you are in full view of them. If you are *with* someone when I click the icon, I get a WAIT sign; it does not activate immediately; it waits until the program judges that you are out of sight of everyone else. That's why I couldn't get you back until you lost your footing and drifted off and away from your sister. With both of you out of each other's sight, I could then get you both back. So that is an important lesson for you to learn. It is important for you to regularly spend time on your own so I can come through to you if I need to. If you are always in other people's company, it can make things difficult for me.'

'That's all very well. But suppose I want to come back before you decide to get me out of there. I decide I've had enough, right? I've checked that I'm out of sight of everyone else – like you said. So, what do I do?' asked Scott.

'You can't do anything,' replied Theo. 'You have to wait until I release you.'

'We just have to wait? We can't decide for ourselves?' frowned Lucie.

'No. Of course not.'

'Why not?'

'For the simple reason that you do not *know* there is another world to come back to. When you are in Virtutopia, that is *the* world – the one and only world – as far as you are concerned. You can't have any inkling that it is just a virtual reality. So it has to be *me* who is in control of when you come back, and *only* me.'

'But suppose you had not been able to get me

back in time?' asked Scott looking worried. 'Did you not just now tell Lucie that I would have drowned. I would *really* have drowned?'

Theo repeated what had earlier been said to the reporters at the press conference a month earlier: the world might be make-believe, but one's inter-actions with it and with other people are not. 'You struck your ankle on a rock which was imaginary,' he told Scott. 'But the suit genuinely damaged your foot. If you had fallen off a cliff and hit your head, the suit could genuinely kill you by what it does to your head. Drown in imaginary water, and the suit will drown you.'

'But how?' asked Scott. 'It has no water in it. It didn't even get wet.'

'Drowning is all about not being able to breathe. The suit would have cut off your air supply; you would have died from a lack of oxygen. It would come to the same thing. Make no mistake about it: Life in this type of virtual reality can be just as damaging and deadly as life in the real world. After all, the world you were in then was an exact copy of this world and the way it operates – so the consequences will be exactly the same.'

Lucie grimaced. 'I don't like the sound of all this.'

'As I told your parents, there are risks associated with the project. That's why they had to sign that waiver form to say that they appreciated the risks you will be running. But the risks are no greater, and no less, than what you would run in the normal way.'

'But they *are* greater,' insisted Lucie. 'I am used to the risks in this world. But as for the other . . . I didn't know anything about tides rushing in like that.'

'Fair enough,' admitted Theo. 'I suppose we just have to say that that was a bit like visiting a foreign country. That too can expose you to unfamiliar hazards, requiring you to take especial care.'

'It's not a very good beginning for a world if you drown everyone in it in no time at all,' muttered Scott.

'This is one of the problems we are going to have to face when we change the nature of the virtual reality – when we deliberately make it different from the world we are familiar with. There are likely to be some unforeseen consequences. That's why we are engaged in this experimental programme – designing different kinds of world and seeing what happens.'

'And another thing,' said Lucie. 'What if there's a power cut while we are in Virtutopia. Will we be all right?'

'We have back-up power supplies,' Theo reassured her.

'But what if the computer system crashes? Dad's always complaining about his computer crashing,' ventured Scott. 'The cybersuits could go out of control and . . . and strangle everyone in Virtutopia.'

'That is *highly* unlikely,' stated Theo.

'But it *could* happen,' insisted Scott.

'I don't see how. But, yes, I suppose there might be a remote possibility of something like that. But then again, that wouldn't be any different to the way things are in this world. Who knows . . . all life might be wiped out tomorrow by a meteorite crashing on to Earth.'

'Like the one that killed off the dinosaurs?' volunteered Scott, eager to show off his knowledge.

'That's right. It's a risk we have to take.'

'Can I ask you something else, Theo?' Lucie ventured.

'Fire away.'

'Well, when we were in the forest, we couldn't recall how we came to be there. Neither of us knew which forest we were in or how we had got there in the first place. Why was that?'

'Ah, yes. Well spotted. That's a bit of a problem we still have. You see, we can't have you remembering what has just happened – because what has just happened is that you have stood on a platform in a laboratory wearing a cybersuit, getting your instructions from me. If you remembered that, then you would immediately know that you were now in nothing more than a virtual reality. The memory would destroy the illusion of reality. We can't allow that. So, we have to eliminate the memory.'

'Eliminate the memory!' exclaimed Lucie, looking alarmed. 'That sounds horrible!'

'As a temporary measure,' the scientist hastened to add. 'That's all it is. What we do – with this particular model – is to short-circuit your short-term memory. Certain of the electrodes in the headset are there for that specific reason. This means you still remember all about who you are, your general background history; that's not affected. But you end up unclear as to how you landed up in whatever location you happen to find yourself in – that forest for instance. Eventually, when we've had more experience, we intend to build up a false memory bank which can be input into your brain so that there will seem to be some plausible reason for how you come to be doing what you are doing in Virtutopia. The false memory will provide you with a bridge from your real history into your virtual existence.'

'I don't like the sound of that either,' protested Lucie. 'I don't want to live with false memories of what has happened in the past.'

'People do it all the time,' Theo murmured to himself; adding aloud, 'But anyway, enough of that. Are you still both willing to help?'

He paused and looked at them anxiously. They nodded – though Lucie somewhat reluctantly.

'Good,' he continued. 'In that case, we might as well make a start. So, what kind of Virtutopian world would you like?'

Lucie looked uncomfortable.

'Something still bothering you, Lucie?' asked Theo.

'Well, you talk about us helping you to design this Virtutopia. But . . . but neither of us has the foggiest idea how all this works,' she said helplessly pointing to the console, the monitor screens, and the racks of electronics. 'What use can we be if we don't know how to work all this?'

Theo laughed. 'Bless you, you don't need to know anything about that side of things. That's the easy part. Just leave that to me. No what I want from you – what I *need* from you – are *ideas*. Ideas about what would make for a perfect, utopian world. We need some overall plan – a plan that sums up what your favourite world would be like – some guiding principle I can follow when I set the thing up.'

Scott brightened up. 'Well, that's easy. A world where everyone is happy,' he said, looking across at Lucie. She nodded in agreement.

'You want everybody to be happy,' repeated Theo slowly and thoughtfully. 'Good. Yes, that sounds good to me. A bit vague, mind you. Hardly what I would call a *plan*. What precisely do you have in mind? What makes for happiness? Have a think about that, and when you have decided, give me a call and I'll see what I can do.'

Scott already had a gleam in his eye.

Five

All You Want

Christmas. The worst time in the whole year, as far as Scott was concerned. 'Here we go again,' he muttered to Lucie as they confronted the mound of presents under the tree. 'Thank you, thank you so much. It's just what I wanted,' he continued in a mocking, sing-song tone of voice.

'Quiet! They'll hear you,' hissed his sister.

'Well . . . You know what I mean. I can't wait for it all to be over and done with. Every year it's the same embarrassing load of nonsense.'

Scott began ripping the wrapping off the presents. The first revealed a stack of CDs. He thumbed idly through them. Dumping them on the ground next to where he was sitting, he declared, 'See what I mean? I've got them. There's not one I haven't got already. Why do they waste their time buying such rubbish – and waste *my* time having to open their stupid parcels? Why can't they ask me what I want instead of just going ahead without consulting me?'

'You know why,' said Lucie holding up a pair of designer jeans she had just unwrapped.

'No, I don't,' he protested.

Lucie thought for a moment, then smiling sweetly and putting on her mother's voice, began, 'Tell me, my dear boy, what CDs would you like for Christmas? Do you have a list I can give Father Christmas?'

'Oh shut up, you,' retorted her brother angrily.

'"Oh shut up you",' repeated Lucie slowly, pretending to write it down. 'And who sings that, my dear?'

Scott picked up the nearest box and threw it at her. It missed, and crashed against the wall. There was the sound of shattering glass.

'Oh, very good, Scott. Now you've done it,' scolded Lucie. 'That was the flower vase Dad was giving Mum.'

'So what? He can always get her another. She's already got one almost identical, anyway. Mum won't be upset. You'll see.'

'That's hardly the point, is it?' replied Lucie. 'The point is that there isn't a single CD in the whole wide world that you want and haven't got. So what's the point of Mum asking you. She might just as well go out and buy one set of CDs as any other. They'll all end up in the bin by tomorrow anyway – along with these,' she added, regarding the jeans she was holding. 'How many of *these* can one person wear? I don't have room to store any more.'

'That's what I mean about the hell of Christmas,' moaned Scott. 'We go through the motions of unwrapping all these presents; we say how wonderful they all are – and then bin the lot. Either that, or we have to throw out tons of stuff we already have just to make room for the new lot of junk. And all the time we have to go on about how thankful we are, and how wonderful it all is.'

They dutifully unwrapped the parcels, stacked up the presents and disposed of the wrapping paper. When they had finished, Lucie got on her mobile.

'Hi, Sharon. Thanks. You too. So, what did you get for Christmas? . . . You can't remember? No, I can't either. Masses of stuff. Always the same, isn't it . . . I did get a new Armani jacket from Mum . . . You too? Yes, I'm having to find room in my wardrobes to put it with the other six or seven of them . . . Twenty!? You have twenty, I see . . . Anyway, I must fly. Haven't had breakfast yet. Good to talk to you.'

Snapping her mobile shut, she muttered something about 'cow' and 'show-off', before going into the kitchen. There she found Scott had already made a start on his breakfast – and was being sick.

'Oh dear,' soothed Mrs Harris. 'I told you only yesterday, darling: chocolate fudge cake and whipped cream for breakfast does not appear to agree with you any more, you poor thing.'

'But it's my favourite,' insisted Scott grumpily.

'I know, dear. You know best. Never mind. You can have some more when you feel a little better.'

After breakfast, Lucie spent the rest of the morning trying to decide which clothes to throw out to make room for the new arrivals – most of those being discarded never having been worn. Scott meanwhile was sprawled in front of the TV set, flicking through the channels.

'It's ridiculous. How am I supposed to find what I want to watch most?' he grumbled.

'I know it's difficult,' agreed his mother. 'They say there will soon be a thousand channels to choose from.'

'There are a thousand already – one thousand and fifty-six, if you must know.'

'And none you like?

'Oh, I like lots of them. But which one I would like *most* – it's so difficult trying to decide. It's all so boring.'

'And how many more times do I have to hear you saying *that*?' demanded his father, irritably.

'Well, it's true.'

'I'm not saying it's not. But I don't know why you bother. You watch too much television as it is.'

'There's nothing else to do,' Scott replied.

'I keep telling you: get a part-time job – evenings or weekends.'

'What's the point?'

'It would get you out of the house. You'd earn some pocket money.'

'What for? I can already buy anything I want.'

'Well,' intervened Mrs Harris, changing the subject, 'I'll tell you what. We'll all take a brisk walk in the sunshine; it will give us an appetite for lunch.'

'I'm afraid you'll have to count me out,' said Mr Harris. 'I have to take the Mercedes for a drive. I haven't been out in it for weeks and the battery will run down if I don't take it for a spin.'

Mrs Harris looked at the clock on the mantelpiece. 'Nearly time for Aunt Kate to arrive.'

She and her husband got up and went out. Together they strolled down the driveway of their palatial home. Cars stretched all the way down the drive to the distant entrance gates to their estate.

'I've often wondered why we have to have so many cars, darling, 'said Mrs Harris. 'It's such a chore for you, poor dear, to have to keep remembering to give each one a run so that they don't get neglected.'

'So many cars, did you say? I wouldn't say that,' he replied airily. 'We only have a dozen or so. Well, perhaps twenty.'

'More like thirty, if you ask me.'

'But everyone needs cars, don't they? You can hardly expect me to be driving the same car every day. Nobody does that. We all need a change.'

'Yes of course, dear. You know best. In fact, I've been thinking. If we tarmacked over that patch of grass there between the house and the first of the garages, you'd have parking space for another.'

'I say, that's a splendid idea. That way we would have space for a Rolls-Royce. I've always wanted a Rolls.'

'Erm . . . I always thought the blue one over there was a Rolls-Royce, dear.'

'What?' asked Mr Harris following her gaze. 'Oh yes. I was forgetting. What a pity. I was looking forward . . . Never mind. I'm sure I can find a nice car I haven't already got.'

Mrs Harris looked sceptical.

'Anyway, we'll get the workers in straight away to do the tarmacking,' continued Mr Harris.

As she spoke, an Audi estate car turned off the road and came down the driveway towards them. It was Aunt Kate. Having no family of her own, Aunt Kate always came to the Harrises' for Christmas lunch. She stopped outside the front door. Mrs Harris called inside to the children to come and help carry the presents. They did their best to put on a show of being thrilled and excited. But in private they knew that Aunt Kate, just like their parents, *never* brought them anything they did not already have.

During lunch, Lucie paused from eating. 'Mum, we haven't got anything for you or for Dad,' she said. 'You were supposed to be telling us what you wanted – but you didn't.'

'I have been thinking, dear. But I simply cannot come up with a single thing . . . I tell you what: why don't you *do* something for us instead? That would make a nice present. You could volunteer to do the washing-up after lunch. That would be ever so helpful.'

Scott frowned. 'You're forgetting. The new dish-washer system. It does everything.'

'Everything? Surely not *everything*,' she laughed. 'You could at least clear the table and load the dish-washer . . . Oh no. That's what that new shute thing does. Anyway, you can empty the dishwasher

afterwards and put the dishes back in the cupboard.'

It was now Lucie's turn to look exasperated. 'But
isn't that what the conveyor belts do? You're thinking of the *old* dishwasher – or the one before that.
This latest model does all that automatically as
soon as the dishes are dry. Puts them back in the
cupboard. Don't you remember? Dad went out
and bought it when you tripped and dropped . . .'

'Oh yes. Sorry,' said Mrs Harris in disappointment. 'You're right. Silly me. No, in that case I
don't know *what* to suggest.'

'Ah. Here comes Daryl,' interrupted Scott looking out of the dining-room window and noticing
his friend coming down the drive. 'What's that dog
he's got with him?'

He went out to greet him. Daryl called out
cheerily, 'Hi, Scott. How do you like him? He's a
Labrador.'

'Yes, I know,' replied Scott. 'We've got one ourselves.'

'This is my *second* – a male and a female,' added
Daryl in a superior tone. 'I now have a complete
collection of mating pairs for all the main breeds of
dog.'

Not to be outdone, Scott replied, 'We got tired of
dogs months ago. We're now into cats: Persian,
Siamese, Abyssinian . . .'

'Cats! Oh, give me a break,' declared Daryl,
dismissively. 'No one collects cats any more. I got

rid of my lot ages ago.' He looked about him. 'Do you mind if I use your back gate and go through the paddock?'

'Not if you keep that thing on a lead and don't frighten our horses.'

Seething inside, Scott accompanied him round the house, deliberately guiding him past the rows of dustbins filled to overflowing with discarded new items. With satisfaction he noticed Daryl eyeing all the goods they were throwing out.

'Come on, Rex,' Daryl commanded, snapping his fingers. And with that, he and his dog passed through the gate and sauntered nonchalantly across the field before disappearing behind the stables.

Six

Less is More

'So. How did it go? What do you reckon?' asked Theo. Scott had just joined him in the control room, having removed his cybersuit in the next door lab. The boy slumped down in the chair next to the scientist. At first he said nothing; he just looked thoughtful and dejected.

'What's the matter?' enquired Theo.

Scott shrugged his shoulders noncommittally. But was still silent.

'You said you wanted to have everything you wanted,' Theo remarked. 'You wanted to be rich – loads of money. Wasn't that enough? Did you need more? You have only to say. You can go back and I'll arrange for you to . . .'

'No, no,' the boy shook his head. 'It was enough. Plenty. It's just . . . Oh, I don't know. It all seemed a bit pointless.'

'Pointless?'

'Yes. You know . . . Nothing to look forward to.'

They both lapsed into silence.

Lucie entered, putting a comb through her hair and patting it into place. 'I was surprised at Sharon,' she began. 'She really upset me. That wasn't like her. I could hardly believe it was her on the phone.'

'Yeah. Daryl was different too,' agreed Scott.

'And Dad,' added Lucie. 'What did he need all those cars for? How many cars can one person be driving at a time!'

'Oh, I don't know about that. Some of those cars were pretty neat,' said Scott.

'Yes, yes, I know they were. But you know what I mean. He was just being greedy. He certainly didn't strike me as though he actually *enjoyed* owning them all.'

'You say they weren't like their normal selves,' said Theo. 'But it was them all right. No doubt about that,' he assured them. 'If you thought they seemed different, then that's because that is what they would be like if they inhabited that sort of

Virtutopia. They couldn't help it – any more than you could.'

'What do you mean "any more than we could"?' asked Lucie, regarding him searchingly.

'Nothing. Just that you too were the sort of person you would have been if you had been brought up in that kind of world.'

'Meaning?' she persisted.

'Meaning . . . I prefer you the way you are – now. The kind of people you are in *this* world.'

He got up and wandered over to the door. Looking through to the lab, he said, 'Oh, no. I'm sorry. This won't do. You mustn't just dump the suits on the floor when you're finished. You've got to remember they are easily damaged. We don't want people falling over them. Come on. Get into the habit of putting them back on their hangers when you're done.'

They followed him into the lab and dutifully did as they were instructed.

'The headset gets put on the shelf above its suit. That's where it belongs. Right?'

They nodded. Scott paused in front of the platforms. 'Why do we use these?' he asked. 'Why do we have to stand on a platform when we go to Virtutopia? Why not just stand on the floor?'

The two platforms lay on the floor side-by-side. They were each about the size of a double bed, with a height of 20 to 25 centimetres.

'You need those for walking or running about,'

Theo explained. 'If you start walking in Virtutopia, that's because the *real* you – you in this room – you've started walking here. But if you did that while standing on the floor, what would happen? You'd bang into that wall over there, right? And that is something the 'you' in Virtutopia would also feel – despite there being nothing in Virtutopia for that 'you' to bang into. And that's it: end of illusion. But on the platform . . . well, I'll tell you what, go ahead and try it. Get up on the platform. No, you don't need your suit this time. Just mount it and stand in the middle. Now wait just a tick.' He popped back into the control room for a moment. On returning he said, 'OK. Go ahead and walk.'

Scott did as suggested and was astonished to find that he got nowhere. The moment he took a step forward the top surface of the platform started to move – rather like a conveyor belt. As he kept walking, the platform kept pace with him so he stayed on the same spot.

'Try running,' suggested Theo. 'Vary your pace.'

Scott found that no matter how hard he ran, he was simply running on the spot. Furthermore, no matter how suddenly he slowed down, or quickened his pace, it made no difference. The platform had the uncanny knack of immediately compensating for any change of speed.

'But what if he changed *direction*?' asked Lucie, clearly intrigued. 'Wouldn't he fall off the side of the platform?'

'You heard what she said, Scott,' said Theo with an amused look on his face. 'Try it.'

Scott veered this way and that way. But to no avail. The platform's motion also changed direction in exactly the same way, so he still remained in the same place at the centre of the platform.

The boy stopped, and stared down at the platform. 'How on earth did it do *that*?' he exclaimed. 'Going in *one* direction, yes. You could do that with a couple of rollers for the belt to go over. But changing direction!'

'That? Oh . . .' sighed Theo. 'That was a nightmare. Fortunately I have this colleague – he's a wizard with anything mechanical. He eventually got it sorted out. Not me. It's still a puzzle to me. You'll have to ask him, if you really want to know.'

'Why do the platforms have to be so big – if we stay in the centre of them all the time?' asked Scott.

'So you can lie down. When you lay down on the beach that first time, or sprawled out on the sofa the second time in Virtutopia, your real self was lying down on the platform here – so it has to be bed-sized. Which is a nuisance. We get quite a number of complaints – from those who have IPVR already; they complain the platforms take up too much space in the home. But we can't see any way round that one.'

He glanced up at the clock on the wall. 'Come on, I need to be locking up for the night.' Starting out for the door, he added, 'By tomorrow you will need to have come up with some other way you might be happy in Virtutopia. It's your turn next, Lucie. Scott's idea didn't work out too well. What kind of Virtutopia do *you* want?'

'Hey, you two,' came an anguished cry from Scott. 'What about me?' They looked back and burst out laughing. Scott was frantically trying to get off the platform, but it wouldn't let him; the movement of the surface kept compensating for his every movement, with the result that he could not get away from the platform.

'I guess we had better leave him there, eh Lucie,' chuckled Theo. 'He asks too many questions anyway.'

Another anguished cry from Scott. Theo relented. 'All right, all right. Keep your hair on. I'll put the clamp back on.'

He returned to the control room, flicked a switch on the console. Joining them once more, he grinned. 'OK. Look sharp. You should be all right now.'

Seven

Best Behaviour

'Here, let me help you with your bag,' said a voice from behind her. Lucie glanced over her shoulder. Oh no. Not Daryl Hibbert!

'It looks heavy,' he added. Without waiting for an answer, he snatched it out of her hand as he came up alongside. Hibbert was a bully. Lucie felt a wave of panic surge through her. He was about to make off with the bag; either that, or he would tip all the contents out onto the pavement. She desperately looked up and down the street for someone to help her. But there was no one near.

'Lots of homework?' he asked.

Lucie nodded dumbly.

'Poor you,' he said with a smile. 'I've been let off lightly tonight – for a change.'

They continued down the road, Lucie's heart pounding as she frantically searched her mind for what he might be up to. But nothing happened. They reached the bus stop.

'Right then,' he said. 'You catch the bus from here, don't you?' Again she nodded. 'I live just round the corner,' he said, placing the bag down carefully. 'Be seeing you, Lucie.' With that he sauntered off, hands in pockets.

'Er . . . 'bye. And, er . . . thank you . . . Daryl,' murmured Lucie in confusion. She was left wondering what on earth that had been about. Was she dreaming?

She didn't have long to ponder this before the bus drew up at the stop. The queue shuffled forward. By the time Lucie got on, there was just one seat left – and that was next to Karen Spencer – a classmate Lucie did not get on with at all. She decided to stand.

'No standing. You know the rules,' called out the driver, eyeing her in his mirror. 'Find a seat somewhere, or you'll have to get off and wait for the next one.'

She reluctantly went and sat next to Karen. Karen looked embarrassed and deliberately stared out of the window.

After they had gone a little way, Lucie turned and quite suddenly asked, 'How are you, Karen? Everything OK?' The words just tumbled out. For one brief moment she thought she must be listening to someone else speaking. But no. It was her own voice. Whatever possessed her to say such a thing – to *her* of all people?

Karen immediately brightened up. 'I'm fine, Lucie. Thanks. Apart from having a bit of a cold. But I'm mostly over that now. How are *you*?'

Lucie nodded. 'Fine.'

Karen began discussing the English lesson they had had that morning. 'I thought it was rubbish,' she said. 'Shakespeare's *Henry V* – it's stupid. Take all that talk about "war". Was that what she called it? "War"? People fighting and killing each other. *Killing* each other! As if anyone would do a thing like that. It was too far-fetched; it was silly. Stories should be about real life – things that actually happen.'

Lucie found herself agreeing with Karen. They became so engrossed in their conversation, she almost missed her stop.

Alighting from the bus, Lucie entered the local supermarket. It was not that she expected to buy anything; she just liked leafing through the CDs to see what was new. As she was doing this, she could not help noticing a boy further along the aisle, standing in front of where the sweets were. What drew her attention to him was his shifty look – the way he was furtively looking about him to see if anyone was watching him. Lucie pretended not to notice. Then all of a sudden, he reached forward and picked up a handful of chocolate bars and stuffed them into his jacket pocket. Lucie didn't know what to do. She supposed the shoplifter would be caught on the security camera. But no. There didn't seem to be a camera – not one in the whole shop. Anyway, she thought, it was none of her business. She just carried on sifting through the CDs.

At last she saw one she wanted. Unfortunately she discovered she hadn't enough money on her. It was Friday and she did not get her allowance until Saturday. She returned the CD to its place, resolving to return the next day.

Making her way to the exit, she found herself behind the boy with the bulging jacket pockets. He was hurrying towards the gangway that bypassed the tills – the one used by those not making a purchase. The thought flashed through her mind: should she tell on him? But she needn't have bothered. Suddenly the boy slowed down – almost as though he had hit a brick wall. He hesitated. He looked about him with an expression on his face that was a mixture of frustration, anger, and bewilderment. Then to Lucie's surprise, he turned and meekly joined the end of one of the check-out queues, pulling the chocolate bars out of his pocket for all to see.

'How very odd,' thought Lucie. 'I could have sworn . . . Ah well. Perhaps I mistook him.'

Out on the street again, she paused momentarily to examine a sleek, low-slung, smart sports car, parked by the side of the road. Its roof was down. The keys, which had been casually left in the ignition, glinted in the sun. It was in fact a lovely sunny afternoon – the sort of afternoon where everyone left their windows and doors wide open.

A little further down the road, she passed the youth centre. Carved into the stone block above the doorway one could still make out that it said Police Station – not that anyone living could remember it having been a police station. Indeed, most people had no idea what the words 'police station' meant.

Turning down a side alley, she walked alongside a smooth, plastered wall, painted white. Not being overlooked, it would have been ideal for graffiti artists to get to work. But it was pristine clean.

A little further on, she was curious to see that someone had placed a wallet on a garden wall – a bulging wallet. It had clearly been put there, much as one might place a glove that had been dropped. But this was not a glove; this was a wallet. Lucie could see a bundle of bank notes peeping out of it. She was dying to take a look. Not to touch the money, of course, but out of curiosity. Except . . . except that there were so many notes, one would hardly be missed. Even if it were, she could blame its theft on whoever found the wallet in the first place. Besides, the owner would be so relieved to get back the bulk of their money, they would hardly kick up a fuss over one miserable £10 note. But £10 would mean she could go back to the shop for the CD. The temptation was too much.

But then a strange thing happened – or perhaps one should say, *didn't* happen. Her hand would not come out of her pocket. She pulled and pulled on it, but it would not budge; it seemed to have been paralysed. Either that, or, so she supposed, she must have been placed in a hypnotic trance. Perhaps a hypnotist had planted a suggestion in her mind. Anyway, for whatever reason, try as she might, she couldn't remove her hand in order to pick up the wallet.

Eventually she gave up, quite baffled. She got back to their little semi-detached home. She opened the garden gate – noting that her hand came out of the pocket with no difficulty at all this time. There was no need for a front door key; the door was ajar, and in any case, there was no lock; people came and went as they pleased.

Scott was already there doing his homework. She reminded him that his favourite TV programme had just started. But he waved her aside and carried on working. 'I'd rather get this out of the way so I don't have it hanging over me all weekend,' he explained.

They had their meal. When they had finished, Scott volunteered to do the washing-up.

'Not again,' laughed his mother. 'You did it at breakfast. You must give Lucie a chance sometime.'

'Yes, yes,' Lucie found herself saying eagerly, with her mouth full. 'It's my turn, remember.'

Mrs Harris beamed at them.

Later that evening, as they settled down to an evening before the fire, Mr Harris looked up from the newspaper he was reading and enquired of the children, 'Now what have you to tell us? A little bird told me on the phone earlier today, that one of you had won an award at school.'

'Both of us actually,' replied Lucie. 'We both won badges for being good and well-behaved.'

Mr and Mrs Harris gave each other a glowing smile. Turning to the children, Mr Harris enthused, 'Really, we are *so* proud of you. Both of you. You are a credit to us.'

Eight

Robots

The staff restaurant was always busy at this time, but Theo and the children had managed to find a table to themselves. Scott was soon tucking in enthusiastically. Lucie, on the other hand, was picking at her food thoughtfully. Eventually she pushed it to one side, and leant back in her chair.

'That was awful. It was . . . too sickly.'

'Sickly?' murmured Theo in surprise. 'I think it tastes rather good.'

'I'm not talking about *that*,' she said pointing with her fork to the plate in front of her. 'I was talking about that last session we've just had.'

'Oh. Why? What was wrong with it?'

'As I say, it was sickly. Everybody being goody-goody.'

'But that was the kind of world you told me you wanted,' said Theo. 'A world with no evil. People only doing good. A world with no war. That has to be good – surely?'

'Ye-es,' agreed Lucie.

'No crime, no prisons, no judges, no police, no security guards, no vandalism, no bullying. That's what you asked for.'

'I know I asked for it. But I didn't think it would

work out like *that*. I wanted people to be *good*. But those people weren't being good. They behaved like that because that was the only way they *could* behave. When I tried to take the money out of the wallet, my hand wouldn't do what I wanted it to do. And I bet the same went for that boy in the supermarket. No way would he have paid for those chocolate bars if he didn't have to. He was forced into it. And if that's what happens when real criminals try to commit a crime, no wonder there's no crime. No wonder you don't need prisons and police and stuff. And as for those stars we won for good behaviour. That was a load of nonsense. *Everyone* in the class won a star for being good. Why? Because we had no alternative; that's why. We *had* to be good. I want to live my own life in the way *I* want. Is that asking too much?'

'But you can't do that,' replied Theo. 'And neither can anyone else.'

'But why?'

'Because you wanted a world without evil. That's what you said. No evil. That automatically meant that any bad or evil intention has to be overridden. The program – the one governing the running of Virtutopia – has to substitute the right action.'

'How does it do that?' asked Scott, with his mouth full.

'It's not difficult,' said the scientist. 'The cyber-suit made sure she couldn't physically move her hand when she tried to take the money that didn't belong to her. The boy's suit marched him off to the check-out till.'

'But what about all that stuff I was saying to Karen, I didn't mean it – not really; it just sort of came out. It didn't feel as though it was the *real* me saying it.'

'Oh, you felt that too, did you?' asked Scott, taking an interest. 'The same thing happened to me. At the end of the lesson, I went up to Mrs Simpson and thanked her. Can you believe that? I actually thanked a teacher! I could hear myself telling her I had enjoyed the lesson and found it very interesting.'

'That must have been some lesson,' said Theo in amusement.

'But that's the point. It hadn't been at all interesting. I was bored out of my skull. But that's what I said. Somehow I couldn't help myself. It just sort of slipped out. So, what was that about?'

'It's all done through the electrodes in the headset. They prompt you to say the right kind of thing – the kind of thing a *good* boy might say.'

'But that's my point!' cried Lucie in exasperation. 'He wasn't being good . . .'

'So, how is it all going?' A booming voice interrupted their conversation. They turned to see the figure of Lord Harsk himself towering above them. He enquired of Theo who the two children were.

'The two guinea pigs I told you about,' replied Theo.

'The what?'

'You know. I mentioned . . .'

'Oh yes. I vaguely remember you saying something of the sort. I didn't realise you were actually going ahead with that daft idea. I distinctly recall telling you it wasn't necessary. We already know what people want from Virtutopia. Anyway,' he added impatiently, 'how are they getting on?'

Theo began by explaining that they had started out with a world where people have everything they could possibly want.

'Hah!' exclaimed the boss, warmly. He sat down in the spare seat at their table. 'Great idea, eh?' he said to the children. They didn't know what to say. They stared fixedly at the tabletop, completely overawed.

'Well . . . in point of fact, *no*,' said Theo, coming to their rescue.

'*No*?' exploded Harsk in a voice that echoed round the entire room, causing others to stop eating and look across at them to see what the fuss was about. 'Not satisfied?' He then muttered something under his breath, which they couldn't quite catch, but that sounded something like 'ungrateful brats'.

'We have moved on from there – to a world without evil.'

'A world without evil,' replied Harsk, calming down once more. 'Very good. Excellent. I take it *that* was to your liking,' he said to the children. 'We are all against evil.'

He was about to get up and move on, when Theo said, 'Not exactly.' Harsk looked thunderstruck.

'We were discussing it just now. They did not like the way they knew that their actions were being censored,' explained Theo. 'They were only able to act in certain ways and say certain types of thing. They were experiencing an inner conflict.'

'Inner conflict, my foot!' barked the boss. 'Teething troubles, that's all it is. Just teething troubles.'

'I agree,' replied Theo submissively. 'I was about to tell them that this was likely to be just a temporary drawback with this particular model.' He turned to the children. 'You see, the electrical signals transmitted to your brain to get you to do and say the right things are doing a good job. Unfortunately there remain certain parts of your brain that are aware that something odd is going on; something is not right. That's when you get to feel that it is not the real you that is speaking and acting that way. It sets up an unfortunate conflict in you.'

'Exactly. A minor glitch,' added Harsk. 'I'm sure you'll get it sorted out in no time, Birkin. As we get to understand which parts of the brain have these disruptive feelings, we shall arrange for them to be short-circuited.'

'Yes, but . . .' ventured Lucie tentatively. 'Surely that would simply turn me into an automaton – a robot. It wouldn't be the real me.'

'The "real me". Pah!' declared Harsk dismissively. 'What makes you so sure you aren't already robots. What you say and do is determined by what your parents and teachers have taught you to say and do. They've *programmed* you.'

'They certainly have not,' replied Lucie gathering courage. 'I am not a copy of my parents. I deliberately do things differently from what they tell me.'

'Me too,' said Scott defiantly joining in. 'Dad supports Arsenal; I support Spurs. Mum goes to church; I don't.'

'Quite the little rebel, aren't we,' sneered Harsk. 'OK. So you are the rebel type. You always do the *opposite* to your parents. It comes to the same thing in the end. Conform or rebel – you are simply what you are in relation to your parents. All we shall be doing in Virtutopia is fixing your personality in a different – and better – way.'

'But it isn't as simple as that,' insisted Lucie. 'Sometimes I agree with my parents, and sometimes not. I make my own decisions; I have a choice whether to do the same as them, or something different.'

'Do you, young lady?' snarled Harsk leaning towards her menacingly. 'What makes you so sure you have a choice? You do your thinking with that, right?' he said tapping her on the forehead. 'Your brain – assuming you've got one in there. Your brain is a lump of matter that is blindly following the dictates of the laws of nature. If I knew everything about your brain at one point in time, I could predict – note that – *predict* what you are going to do next. Which means I could predict what the outcome of your so-called "choice" will be. There's no choice involved at all. It is all determined in advance. You are already nothing but a robot, as you put it.

'Besides,' he continued in a more relaxed manner, 'it might not come to that. We might not have to short-circuit parts of your brain. As you get used to the Virtutopian way of life, you will automatically find yourselves conforming your behaviour to its requirements. It will become second nature for you to act only in ways acceptable to the system. You will come to recognise that it is for the best. After a while, all feelings of conflict will melt away, and it won't even occur to you to act differently.'

'But that's brainwashing,' said Lucie, not to be outdone. 'Again, it won't be the real me.'

'If you are doing what you *want* to be doing, then as far as I am concerned that is the real you – regardless of how you come to be wanting those particular things – whether it's because of upbringing, brain short-circuiting, or brainwashing.'

He turned to Theo. 'I suggest you short-circuit this investigation of yours, Birkin. We don't want to waste any more of the firm's time and money, do we.'

An assistant came up to Harsk's elbow and whispered something in his ear. Harsk nodded. Turning back to the others again he said, 'Must be going. Important foreign visitors waiting for me.'

With that he rose, and followed the assistant across the main restaurant to the door leading to the private dining room.

Once he was out of earshot, Lucie muttered, 'What an absolutely disgusting, horrible man he is.'

'And his breath smelled awful,' added Scott.

'That's not very kind,' said Theo. But they noticed he could hardly suppress a smile. 'Anyway,' he continued, 'did he convince you?'

'About what?' asked Lucie.

'About you not being able to make choices – real choices – because of the way you've been brought up by your parents, or because of the way your brain works?'

Lucie thought for a moment. 'I don't know how to explain it, but I still think I am free to make choices and be myself – my true self. Life wouldn't make sense otherwise, would it?'

Theo nodded. 'I agree with you. Don't ask me how it comes about. But like you I believe we have free will; that's what it is called: free will – the ability to decide and make choices over what we do and say. But it also follows that if we are free, some people will abuse that freedom and be evil.'

'But if they are not free – like back there in the lab just now – then, not only are people not evil, they can't be good either – not *genuinely* good. Being good is when you have the possibility of being evil, but you decide not to be. You have a choice, and you make the right choice.'

'What do you think, Scott?' asked Theo.

Scott was studying his empty plate, thinking of something entirely different. 'I don't understand. When I was in Virtutopia just then, I had a meal. It felt like I was eating and drinking as normal; afterwards I wasn't hungry and thirsty any more. But as soon as I got back here, I *was* hungry all over again. What's that all about?' he asked.

'There's no mystery,' explained Theo. 'You don't actually eat anything in Virtutopia; the food is all virtual. It's the electrodes attached to the skull that send signals to make you think you are eating and no longer feeling hungry. But when you get beamed back, things go back to normal – so if you actually are in need of food, you will suddenly feel peckish. This is something we are working on. In the next upgrade we shall incorporate a way of actually arranging for you to take in food of some kind so that you can stay longer in Virtutopia. With things as they are, your stays have to be limited – otherwise you would starve.'

Scott looked thoughtful. 'Is it the same for going to the toilet? Is that virtual too?'

Theo nodded. 'That's something else we have to work on.'

Scott's eyes widened. 'In that case, if you ever see me in Virtutopia hopping from one leg to the other, beam me out quick – before I mess up my suit!'

Nine

Top Dog

Grade A! How about that! Scott was delighted. With much pride he showed his exam paper to the boy next to him. The boy had also been awarded Grade A. And not just the boy, but also the girl next to him on his other side. In fact everyone had been awarded Grade A – absolutely *everyone* in the class. Scott felt deflated.

That afternoon was Sports Day. Scott was in the 100-metre sprint. The gun was fired, and off they went. He ran his heart out and was thrilled to breast the tape. He had won!

So why were they congratulating Harry? he wondered. He quickly learned that it had been a dead heat. Scott was mildly disappointed at the thought that he would have to share the honour with Harry. But still, that did not detract from the fact that he had won. But worse was in store. It wasn't just Harry. All six had dead-heated – they had all breasted the tape at the same instant. They had all won.

Meanwhile, in another part of the sports field, Lucie was competing in the high jump. She was jubilant at beating her personal best. That should be enough to win the prize, she thought. And it

was. The only trouble was all the entrants managed to jump the same height, and all failed at the next. They had all to share first prize.

Clutching her certificate, she got chatting with Stuart. He too had had a successful afternoon, having won the long jump (along with everyone else competing in that event). Lucie had always fancied Stuart. So she could hardly believe her ears when he asked her for a date.

'Well, I don't know,' she replied, heart thumping. 'I'm pretty busy.' She fished out her diary, and indeed most dates were filled – with different boys' names. They agreed on Thursday of the following week.

'Great!' said Stuart. 'You don't know what this

means to me. I've had this thing about you since the first time I saw you. I can hardly believe that at last I have summoned up the courage to ask you out – and you have said yes. I can't wait until Thursday.'

Lucie was ecstatic. What a catch! Stuart of all people. Except, on the way home she got to thinking that she also felt the same way about Chuck, Wayne, Steve – in fact all the boys in her class. Some day she would have to make up her mind which one to go for. But how was she going to choose when she felt equally attracted to them all? She was confused.

That evening she casually mentioned to Scott that Stuart had asked her out. Her brother was utterly unimpressed; he was busy studying last Saturday's football scores: all draws. Eventually he put them to one side.

'Stuart, did you say? Stuart Henderson? Now, let me guess,' he said mischievously. 'Yes, how about: "You don't know what this means to me", "At last I have summoned up the courage . . . ", etc. etc.'

Lucie looked thunderstruck.

'I've heard it all before,' continued Scott carelessly.

'How?' asked his sister indignantly.

'It's his standard chat-up line. It's what he says to *all* the girls.'

'He never does! How can you possibly know that?'

'Phil tells me. Stuart's brother Phil. Know him?

Anyway, Phil's in my class. He reckons you – and possibly that Jenny girl – must be the last ones in the entire school Stuart had yet to get round to. Except that he seems to have added your scalp today.'

Lucie was not the only one in the Harris household that evening who was fuming. Mr Harris came home in a foul temper.

'Can you believe it: another meeting and we're still no closer to a decision,' he declared to his wife as he took off his coat. 'I told them we simply *cannot* go on like this. The equipment is breaking down just about every day now. There's nothing else for it. We have to invest in a completely new and up-to-date rig. Our customers know it; they're leaving us in droves. I don't blame them. When they place their orders with us, they need to know they won't be let down.'

'Yes, dear, I'm sure you're right,' replied Mrs Harris soothingly. 'Did they take your point? Did they see what you were getting at?'

'Oh yes. They all agree with me. No doubt about that.'

'Well, dear, that's good, isn't it? I guess they'll be taking your advice and getting on with it then.'

'I very much doubt it.'

'Oh. And why is that?'

'The usual reason. Someone has to take the lead. Someone has to make a decision and act on it. But there isn't anybody. There's nobody in charge;

there's no one to say, "Right, this is what we do. I take responsibility. The buck stops with me."'

'Ah yes,' said she. 'The old story.'

'Too right. The old story. It doesn't matter what – running a business, running the railway, running a school, running the country – everybody is equally responsible for making all decisions – meaning *nobody* is responsible – and nothing ever gets done. Honestly, I don't know where it's all going to end.'

'Then, dear, why don't *you* take charge? she suggested.

'*Me*? Why me, for heaven's sake? Whatever gave you that idea?' he laughed.

'Why not you? Someone has to.'

'But why *me*?'

'Because . . . well, I'm not sure . . .'

'Exactly. What would George say if I were suddenly to start issuing orders and making decisions? He's just as well qualified as I am to do that. And Henry . . . and Charles . . .'

'Yes, I know, dear. But *somebody* has to be in charge.'

'I agree. But how are we to decide who? We are all equally qualified. There's no way to *choose*.'

Ten

Winning – and Losing

'Row P, seats 54 and 55,' said Theo consulting the
tickets. 'This looks like it. Excuse me. Thank you.'
They pushed past others and found their places.

Sitting down, Scott looked about him excitedly.
'I've never been to a Premier League match before.'

'No, it's quite a treat for me too,' said Theo.
'Someone I know had these two spares. Sorry
about Lucie, but I could only get the two. She's got
some kind of hockey tournament on today anyway
– is that right?'

Scott nodded. 'She wouldn't have come anyway.
She hates football. Storms out of the room whenever
I have it on TV. She says she can't stand all the
deliberate fouling that goes on, diving in the penalty
area, shirt-tugging, swearing at the referee.'

'Can't say I blame her,' Theo said. He looked at
his watch. 'Still twenty minutes to go. We made it
in good time. So, Scott, what did you make of that
last session – back at the lab?'

'That? It didn't work out. It wasn't what I asked
for.'

'No?' said Theo in surprise. 'I thought it was.
What was wrong with it?'

'I wanted to be top. I like winning and being the

best at whatever I do. That really gives me a kick – makes me happy. That's what I asked for.'

'But you *were* top – top of the class. And you won your race.'

'But so did everyone else.'

'Of course. You wanted a world where you were always the winner – you always came out top. That was the plan – the same plan as had to apply to everyone else as well; they must all come top in everything they do. That way there are no losers; no one is unhappy because no one is second-best.'

Scott was not convinced.

'As I've told you before, Virtutopia is not a *game*,' Theo continued. 'It is not peopled by pretend aliens just waiting for you to zap them. It is not a fantasy land swarming with creatures whose sole purpose is to lose to you – leaving you always as the outright winner. Virtutopia is a *reality* – you are interacting with people – *real* people – people who have the same rights as yourself. If we incorporate a rule that you must never be beaten at anything, then that same rule applies to them; they too must never be beaten.

'Take Stuart. He made out that he fancied Lucie. And he genuinely *did* fancy her. But we can't have Lucie winning out over the other girls. That would only upset the other girls. So Stuart has to fancy the other girls as well; he must like them – indeed, love them – just as much as he does Lucie. The same went for Lucie herself. She was equally drawn to

80

all the other boys at school. She could not decide which one she preferred. She preferred them all.'

'Yes, I know that,' said Scott irritably. 'But it's all very well. Lucie hated being just one of a crowd. And what's more she wasn't keen on the idea of fancying every boy she meets. That's not *love*, she told me. It has to be one boy for one girl. Something special between the two of them.'

'I agree with her. But if she is to be singled out by him as being someone *special*, then that will mean other people are going to have to lose out; they are going to be rejected by him – and they won't like it; they'll be unhappy. The same applies to her. If she wants to be in there with a chance of being singled out as someone special, she will have to run the risk of being made unhappy by the many people who will *not* single her out.'

'Well, I don't know about that. That's Lucie's problem. What about those exam results? We all got A grades. What's the good of that?'

'Everyone equally intelligent. All doing well in exams. Why not?' Theo asked. He regarded Scott thoughtfully. 'You know what? It seems to me you didn't really want a Virtutopia where you could do well; you wanted one where you could do *better* than everyone else. You wanted other people to *lose*. And that's not something I can allow. I can't have one rule for you and another for everyone else. Can I?'

Scott shrugged. 'I suppose not,' he conceded

grudgingly. 'And what was all that stuff Dad was going on about?'

'Same sort of thing really. Everybody equal; everybody the boss; everybody in charge – *meaning* nobody's the boss, and nobody is in charge, and no one is in a position to make decisions. Your Dad was having to operate in *your* Virtutopia – the world where everyone is equal. Of course, normal life doesn't work like that. Take this for example,' he said opening the programme at the page listing the teams. 'These players here are in the starting line-up, while these here are on the substitutes' bench. Who decided on that? Someone had to decide; you can't have seventeen men on the field when only eleven are allowed.'

'The manager,' said Scott.

'Yes. The manager. He's in charge. He is the number-one man. Bully for him. But for every successful manager, there must be dozens and dozens of ex-football players who would love to run a big club like this. But they don't; they are disappointed; they're unhappy. This is the one guy with all the prestige, fame, and the hefty pay packet,' he says, pointing to the name of the manager. 'He is the lucky one – until he gets sacked – which I reckon, on their recent form, will be next week. Then it will be his turn to be unhappy.'

'But you have to have a manager, don't you – even though it might upset lots of other people.'

'Careful,' warned Theo with a smile. 'You seem to be voting for a world of winners and losers – a world that might be thought at times to be unfair.'

Changing the subject, Scott asked whether the people he met up with in Virtutopia were real, or just virtual, make-believe people.

'Yes, they're real,' replied Theo. 'Well . . . not exactly – not at the present time. No. At this stage they are make-believe because we are simply try- ing out the various kinds of system. But once we have decided on the system – what kind of Virtutopia is best – then we shall open it up to the public at large. From then on, all the people you will be meeting in Virtutopia will be others on the Internet linked to you via IPVR – people using cybersuits like you. The make-believe characters you have met so far are just temporary. Mind you, they are behaving in exactly the same kind of way as the real people will be doing eventually . . .

'Look,' Scott interrupted. 'The teams are coming out!'

'So they are. At last,' Theo grinned. 'This should be good. Except we already know the result. That rather spoils the excitement.'

'We know the result?'

'Of course. A draw.'

Scott frowned. 'What makes you think that? It might not be.'

'No?' said Theo with a twinkle in his eye. 'Oh no, you're right. I was forgetting. This is not Virtutopia. That should make it more exciting. Of course, if it's not certain to be a draw, we might end up losing.'

'Lose? Us *lose*? Not a chance,' asserted Scott confidently.

'By the way,' asked Theo, 'before they start: have you any idea what Lucie has in mind for the next version of Virtutopia? It's her turn next.'

'No. Well . . . I don't know,' replied Scott casually. He was now concentrating on what was happening down on the pitch. 'She's been complaining about toothache. Said she'd get rid of toothaches and pain next time round. Whether she was serious . . .'

'No pain?' murmured Theo. 'That might be interesting.'

Eleven

Painless

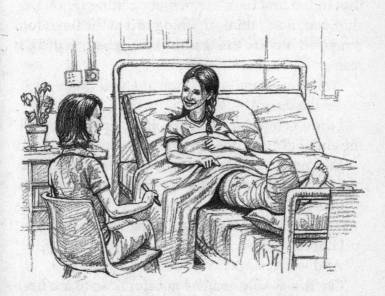

The card said: *To Tracy. Get well soon. Lots of love, the Gang.*

Tracy was Lucie's friend and team-mate. She had broken a leg playing hockey and was in hospital. Lucie was visiting her. She had handed over the card and chocolates, and had added her signature to the plaster cast round Tracy's leg. They were deep in conversation, when the doctor arrived at the bedside. Lucie took the hint and left them to it, wandering down to the far end of the ward.

The doctor consulted the X-rays. 'It's a bad one,

I'm afraid,' he said shaking his head slightly. 'A multiple fracture. Broken in several places. How did it happen?'

'I'm not absolutely sure,' said Tracy. 'I think it was in the first half. I remember getting hit on the shin, but didn't think anything of it at the time. Too wrapped up in the game, I suppose. I didn't realise.'

'And how soon after that did you come off?' asked the doctor.

'I didn't come off,' Tracy replied. 'I played on till the end. I didn't know anything was wrong.'

'You mean . . . you played the whole of the second half with a broken leg! No wonder it's shattered in so many places.'

Lucie meanwhile found herself next to another girl in bed.

'And what happened to you?' she enquired.

'Oh, it was silly, really. I got too close to the fire. My skirt caught alight. It wasn't until it was well on fire that I noticed the smell – the smell of burning flesh – *my* flesh! There's no skin left on the backs of both legs. They plan to do grafts. I'm going to be in here for weeks – perhaps months.'

An orderly arrived with the evening meal. It was time for the visitors to leave. Lucie went back and said a quick goodbye to Tracy. Leaving the ward, she walked down the corridor – slowly, so she could sneak a look into the side rooms. She intended to become a nurse one day and so was interested to see everything she could. She paused at the door of an office. A doctor was sitting there talking with some student doctors and nurses. She couldn't help overhearing.

'That's three we've lost in the past twenty-four hours,' said the doctor, leafing through the files on his lap. 'Sonya Evans. We reckon it must have been food poisoning. She told us she had eaten some berries she found in the hedgerow – red ones. We can't be sure which type until the post-mortem – but they must have been pretty deadly. If only there was some way of telling which foods were good for us and which were poisonous. Something about the taste perhaps – to warn us it is harmful – a kind of bitterness that puts you off from eating any more. But that, of course, is just wishful thinking.

'Damian Runnels - that was only to be expected. He'd lost too much blood from the cut before he noticed anything was wrong. Passed out in the ambulance. We tried blood transfusions, but he never regained consciousness.

'And then Susan O'Donnell. Burst appendix. The usual problem. Never any advance warning when things go wrong with the appendix – or with any of the other internal organs. Out of sight, out of mind, I'm afraid – until it's too late.

'So, that's today's tally. At least it frees up three beds.'

Twelve

Opportunity

It was night-time, and raining. Theo was driving the children back home after their latest session in the laboratory. The rhythmic flip-flop of the windscreen wipers had lulled Scott to sleep on the back seat.

Lucie suddenly pulled a face and held her cheek. Theo looked across.

'Another twinge?' he asked.

She nodded.

'You really must do something about that. Ring up the dentist . . .'

'Mum has,' she replied crossly. 'I'm seeing him nine o'clock tomorrow morning.'

'I'm glad to hear it.'

The conditions were worsening. The rain was turning to sleet.

'Oh yes. I meant to ask you,' said Theo, 'did you feel any toothache when you were in Virtutopia just now?'

Lucie thought for a moment. 'No. No, I didn't, as a matter of fact. That was the one good thing about that visit. How did you manage that? How did you stop the toothache?'

'Oh it's nothing. I had a signal go to your brain to block out all pain.'

'It can block out *real* pain – not just the virtual type you get from what we do in Virtutopia?'

'Of course. There's no difference between what you call "real" and what goes on in Virtutopia. Virtutopia is *real* – it's a reality – it's as real as . . . as *this* world,' he said gesturing around him.

'Well, where toothache is concerned, I'd prefer to be in Virtutopia any day.'

Theo smiled.

After a while, Lucie added, 'Actually . . . probably not. I suppose the toothache was telling me my teeth need fixing. In fact,' she looked searchingly across at Theo, 'that's what that session was all about, right? Pain can be useful.'

Theo nodded. 'A bit of pain at the right time . . .'

'A *bit* of pain, yes,' she interrupted. 'But not all pain. Granddad's arthritis, for example. He has to put up with a lot of pain. But it's not as though it's useful. There's no cure for arthritis. And even with toothache – why does it have to hurt *so much*? A bad tooth is hardly life-threatening! OK, the toothache delivers its warning that something's wrong, Mum rings up for an appointment to see the dentist. And that's it. The pain has done its job. So what's the point of it still nagging on like this?' she said, holding her cheek.

'Oh come on, Lucie,' protested the scientist. 'How is your tooth supposed to *know* that you have an appointment?'

'Well, what about childbirth? Why does that

have to be painful? Answer me *that*.'

But Theo was no longer listening. He was peering intently through the windscreen. Further down the road, there were flashing blue lights. He slowed down as they approached the site. There had been an accident. A white hatchback car was on its side, the front of it buried in the hedge. Nearby, there was a deep gash down the trunk of a tree, presumably caused by impact with the car.

Paramedics, in luminescent yellow jackets, were gathered round. One was on top of the car, reaching in through the open passenger door – trying to get to the driver. There was already someone on a stretcher – presumably a passenger. He or she –

they couldn't tell which – was being eased into the ambulance out of the driving sleet.

'What are we stopping for?' asked Scott, rousing himself. 'Oh,' he said looking out at the scene they were passing. 'What happened?'

'Probably skidded. It's very wet and slippery,' replied Theo.

Once they had gone past, they speeded up once more – but not as fast as they had been going. They lapsed into thoughtful silence. Scott dozed off again.

'I'm hoping to be a nurse one day,' Lucie announced.

'Good. Good for you. Why do you want to be a nurse – if you don't mind my asking? They don't get paid much, you know.'

'Everyone knows that. That's not the point. Nurses and doctors help people – people who are suffering.'

After another quiet spell, Theo asked, 'Ever wondered what it would be like to live in a world where there was *no* suffering? By that I don't just mean no pain; I mean a world where there was no suffering at all – mental as well as physical?'

Lucie looked at him as though she didn't understand what he was getting at.

Theo continued, 'Well, for instance: How would you ever be able to show someone that you loved them if there were never any opportunities to care for them, do things for them, sacrifice yourself for them?'

91

'You could make love to them!' It was Scott. He was wide awake again.

'Sure, Scott. Making love is enjoyable – as you will doubtless find out one day. People get pleasure from it. And that's the trouble with making love. Are you doing it out of genuine love, or are you just having a good time at the other person's expense? How are they to know?' The boy was silent.

'If, on the other hand, you put yourself out for them,' he continued, 'visit them when they're ill, do chores for them when they can't manage; when you are caring and helpful and self-sacrificing, then that's another matter. The other's need is your opportunity to show what you really feel about him or her.'

They pulled up outside the Harrises' home.

'Incidentally, I had a memo from the boss today. He's getting really jumpy. I've stalled him – I left him an answer-phone message that we were making good progress.' Theo glanced across at Lucie and whispered, 'I had my fingers crossed at the time. But seriously, we need to be coming to a decision soon. We can't stall him for ever. So,' he called out to Scott, 'what are we going to be trying out next?'

Scott shrugged. 'Oh I don't know. Why don't we just play it by ear?'

'What does that mean? I have to know what I'm supposed to be programming into the system for tomorrow.'

'Don't program anything. Why don't we just go

to Virtutopia, and once we are there, we decide on the spur of the moment what we want – to suit whatever situation we happen to find ourselves in. We could use our mobile phones. We've both got one. Yes, that would do it. All we need is a helpline – a number to ring up to put in our orders – er . . . our requests. So whenever we want something, we dial up this number and someone – meaning you, Theo – steps in and alters things on demand.'

Theo looked extremely doubtful. 'Well, I don't know about that. Sounds most irregular.'

'So what?' said Lucie, warming to the idea. 'That's the trouble with Virtutopia – and this world as well. Too many rules and regulations. It's all too rigid. There's no flexibility. Yes, Scott. That's a great idea. What would be a good number to call up? Something easy to remember. How about the letters A-S-K? What would that be as a number?'

She consulted her mobile. 'Yes. A is 2, S is 7, and K is 5. So that's it. We dial up 275 and *bingo* – Theo grants our request.

Theo appeared horrified by the suggestion. 'Now hold on, you two. Change the rules just to suit you?'

'Why not? You interfere with Virtutopia every time you want to withdraw us from that world – whenever it suits you. So why not interfere with it when it suits *us*? Don't tell me you *can't* change the rules.'

'Of course I can change the rules,' he declared

indignantly. 'It's *my* virtual world; I set up the rules in the first place.'

'Great! So that's settled,' said Scott.

'Well . . . I don't know,' said Theo frowning. 'Sounds messy to me. I'll have to treat everyone the same – they must all have access to the helpline. You know I have to treat everyone the same.'

'Yes, yes. No problem. Mobiles aren't expensive these days. What's the fuss about?'

'Expense was the last thing I was thinking about . . .' replied Theo with a slight shake of his head.

Thirteen

275

Scott awoke to the inviting smell of fried bacon and eggs. He reached over and pulled back the curtains. Raining. The sheep in the next field looked bedraggled and forlorn.

'Oh *really*!' he exclaimed angrily. He leant out of bed and rummaged through his clothes strewn carelessly over the floor. He fished out his mobile phone.

'2 . . . 7 . . . 5 . . . Hi!. It's me. Scott. Cut it out, will you, Theo. The rain. We're supposed to be on holiday, remember?'

Even as he was speaking, the clouds began to break up, the rain eased off, and the sun began shining through.

'That's better – a lot better. Thanks . . . What?' He scanned the sky. 'Oh yes . . . yes. I can see it. Nice touch. Thanks.' For a while he admired the rainbow, but then began dressing. He slipped his swimming trunks on before putting on his jeans, slicked back his hair, and joined the others in the caravan's kitchen/dining room area for breakfast.

'Good morning, dear. You slept well. Must be the sea air,' called out his mother from the stove. 'Help yourself to cereal; your breakfast is almost ready.'

'Here. You can sit in my place,' said Lucie. 'I've finished.' She got up from the table and disappeared off to the sitting area. Switching the TV on, she settled down on the sofa. It was a news bulletin. Normally she did not watch the news, but this was different. It showed people huddled on the ground, unbelievably haggard and thin. A woman was holding a baby; it was all skin and bone and covered in flies. The reporter was kneeling next to the child. 'If food does not arrive by today, this little one will not see tomorrow,' he said.

Lucie felt sorry for the poor little mite. She always did feel distressed by pictures of people starving. She sometimes wondered whether – once she was a trained nurse – she ought to go out and help victims of famine. But then she suddenly brightened. 'Of course,' she murmured. Getting up, she went and fetched her mobile from the bedroom. 'Can you do something about this, Theo?' she asked. 'These people on the TV . . . What? . . . Er . . . Well, how about turning the rocks into bread? That should do it.'

No sooner had she said this than a look of alarm came over the reporter's face. 'Hey! What's going on? I'm sinking. The ground's gone soft. I can't believe it. It looks like . . . Yes, I am standing on bread!'

The people around him were going wild with delight. They were surrounded by unlimited supplies of bread! They all began tucking in.

Lucie smiled in satisfaction. That was her good deed for the day. But then she began to notice something else. In the background, the buildings belonging to the village, were slowly sinking; they were toppling, and breaking up. Screams could be heard. People were running, terrified, out onto the road. They looked on helplessly as their homes collapsed all around them.

Lucie watched the scene in alarm. 'Oh no!' she exclaimed. 'I didn't mean *all* the rocks to change.' She quickly switched off the TV, horrified at what she had done.

Scott, meanwhile, was finishing his breakfast. 'How far is it to the sea?'

'Well, according to Farmer Thompson, it's a ten-minute walk,' said his father.

'Who's Farmer Thompson?'

'The owner – the one renting the caravan to us. But he did say there was a bus from the end of the lane.'

'I vote we get the bus,' said Scott firmly.

Collecting his beach things from the bedroom, he went outside to wait for the others.

'Oh no. Not again,' he muttered. It was raining once more. He got back onto his mobile, this time pointing out that he wanted sunshine *all day*, not just for five minutes. The clouds dutifully dispersed as before.

'So it was *you*!' bellowed a voice from behind him. He jumped out of his skin. 'I thought as

much. What do you think you are up to?' It was
the farmer's wife. Without waiting for him to
reply, she whipped out her own mobile and
tapped out 2 . . . 7 . . . 5 . . . 'Mrs Thompson here.
Ignore that last call from the boy,' she commanded.
Standing legs apart, hands on hips, she made an
imposing figure. 'I don't know where you come
from,' she continued, 'but wherever it is, you are in
the *country* now. And that's what matters. This is
where the food you eat is grown,' she said, gesturing
to the fields around them. 'It doesn't grow on
supermarket shelves, you know. It grows in fields
– and it needs rain. Do you understand? *Rain*! This
stuff,' she said, holding out her hand as the spots of
rain recommenced.

At this point, Scott's parents came hurrying out

to investigate the commotion. 'You holidaymakers are all the same,' declared Mrs Thompson. 'No consideration. I told my husband no good would come from hiring out caravans. But he wouldn't listen . . .'

Mr and Mrs Harris apologised profusely for any inconvenience caused by their son, and after lengthy discussions, they came to an arrangement. It would rain until noon; then there would be sunshine for the rest of the day.

It was annoying for the family to have to sit around and watch the rain all morning, but sure enough, at 12 o'clock precisely, the sun came out and they were able to make their way to the bus stop.

'How often does the bus go?' asked Lucie.

'No idea,' said Mrs Harris. 'There doesn't seem to be a timetable.'

'We don't need one,' intervened Mr Harris with a grin. 'There's no need to *wait* for a bus.'

With that he got on to his mobile, and requested a bus to appear without delay. The response was immediate: a bus promptly rounded the corner. As soon as it came to a halt, the doors opened, and the driver called out cheerily, 'Hurry along, please.' But to their astonishment, before they had time to take a step forward, the doors slammed to, and the bus lurched forward, disappearing off into the distance in a cloud of dust.

'What got into him?' exclaimed Scott. 'He didn't give us a chance . . .'

'Probably no fault of his. Someone else down the road must have 275'd it. Never mind, it can't be far, and it is a lovely day so we'll walk.'

It wasn't a ten-minute walk as they had been told; it was more like twenty. But eventually the road began to slope down towards the sea, and at last they found themselves on the beach.

'Oh dear,' commented Lucie. 'The tide's in.'

The water was right up to the rocks. But another 275 call from Scott quickly cured that problem; the tide promptly receded into the distance, revealing a fine stretch of sandy beach. Unfortunately the sand remained very wet. Yet another 275 call: 'Make the water less wet please,' asked Scott.

This time the response was not immediate. They waited . . . and waited. Scott knelt down and gathered up a handful of sand. It was still dripping wet. Puzzled, he took out his mobile again. It was showing a text message: *Sorry. Invalid command. Error 137.*

He asked his father what it meant, but Mr Harris shrugged and said he hadn't come across it before.

'Not that it matters,' said Mrs Harris breezily. 'We have a waterproof sheet.'

They laid out the sheet, arranged the fold-up chairs, and settled down for a peaceful afternoon.

'At last,' murmured Mr Harris, lolling back and placing his sun-hat over his face. 'This is the life.'

Lucie and her mother carefully applied suntan lotion. The sun was actually very hot now, blazing down from a cloudless sky.

It was only now Scott noticed that the beach, stretching away to the horizon, was glinting with flashes of silver. At first he could not think what they might be. He was about to ask, when it occurred to him what was causing them: fish. The sun reflecting from silver fish as they writhed and twitched and gasped their last – caught by the sudden removal of the water.

And that was not the only thing out there on the beach. Two people – a man and a woman – who had until then been enjoying a cruise on the open sea, without warning now found themselves firmly grounded on the sand. Even at that distance, Scott could see they were furious. Moreover, from the way they were gesticulating in his direction, it was pretty clear they knew who had been responsible for the plight in which they found themselves. Then, as Scott watched, he could see the man put something to his ear. Moments later, the sea came rushing back.

'Move, move,' cried Mrs Harris, as she frantically tried to gather up her things. The waves came pounding towards them as they scrambled onto the rocks above the high tide level. (Scott vaguely recalled something similar to this having happened to him before – but he could not quite place it.)

Unhappily, the tide reappeared so quickly that they did not have time to rescue all their belongings. The chairs and some of the towels were now floating in the water. Meanwhile, in the distance they could see that the boat had been duly lifted up off the sand once more.

'Right, mate. Two can play at that game,' muttered Scott angrily. He got on the mobile again – and the tide promptly receded. Only this time, it swept the floating chairs and towels out to sea with it – which he had not intended. More seriously, the violence of the out-rushing water had this time caused the boat to tip over as it grounded, throwing the man and woman out.

'Serves them right,' said Scott with satisfaction. The man, dripping wet, stood up and glared in fury at the beached boat – which was now upside down. He was quickly back on the phone. But not for long. He looked at the phone, gave it a bang, and then threw it away; the water had obviously ruined it. He let out an anguished cry, spun round and scowled in the direction of Scott. He shook his fist, and shouted something they could not make out (but it was obviously not meant to be pleasant). With that, he began charging across the sands towards them, splashing through puddles, the woman yelling after him, 'That's it, Joe. Get the nasty little creature. *Vandal*!'

Scott was alarmed. He turned and started scrambling up the rocks. Higher and higher he went. All the time, the man in hot pursuit was gaining on him. Still higher went Scott. He reached the summit and ran and ran, only to find, to his dismay, that his way was cut off by a sheer drop; he was standing on the edge of a cliff. There was no way to go. The man was almost upon him. What should he do? If he jumped, he would be dashed to pieces on the rocks below. If he stood his ground, goodness only knows what would become of him.

'Ah!' he exclaimed. A 275 call. 'Quick, Theo! Make gravity ten times weaker'. Without waiting for a response, he jumped into the abyss. The air rushed past him. Down, down, down. The beach below hurtled towards him. Suddenly, panic seized him as he realised that he was falling at the normal rate – he was definitely not floating down as expected. He shot a glance at the mobile he was still clutching. 'Oh no,' he cried. The screen said: *Sorry. Invalid command. Error 137.*

Fourteen

Dependable

The next thing Scott knew, he was lying spread-eagled, face down. The impact? He did not recall any impact. Perhaps he had passed out on the way down. But the main thing was: he was still alive!

The surface he was lying on felt strange. It was flat and smooth – not at all jagged as you would expect rocks to be. Opening his eyes, he found that he was lying on the platform in the laboratory.

Strong hands grabbed his shoulders and he was turned over onto his back. Theo unclipped the headset and removed it. 'You OK?' he asked anxiously. Scott gave a slight nod and sat up. Theo breathed a sigh of relief, and squatted on the floor beside him.

'That was a narrow squeak,' he murmured.

'What happened?' asked Scott. 'I thought I'd had it. How come I'm back here?'

'How do you think?'

Scott thought for a moment. 'But I don't get it. You must have removed me from Virtutopia while I was still falling. I was in full view of that man chasing me. He must have seen me disappear into thin air. I thought you never did that. You told me it would spoil the illusion – of being in a real world – having people suddenly appearing and disappearing in front of you.'

'Yes, that's the rule – normally – in a *sensible* world. But in the madhouse world you dreamt up there, what's the difference? What's one more crazy thing after all the others you had going on. So – just this once – I overruled that part of the program. But don't bank on me intervening like that next time.'

'Oh there won't be a next time – not in that kind of Virtutopia.'

'Oh. And why not?' asked Theo, with a slight twinkle in his eye.

Scott shrugged and sighed. 'Oh, I don't know.

It . . . well, it was a bit of mess. At first I thought it was going to be real neat, getting the sun to come out, getting the tide to go out, that sort of thing. But the other people kept ruining it – making their own 275 calls.'

'Of course,' replied Theo. 'Why shouldn't they? It's not *your* world; it's not for your exclusive use. Others have exactly the same rights over Virtutopia as you have.'

Scott nodded miserably.

'Which reminds me,' Theo said, glancing across at the suit-clad figure on the other platform. Lucie was determinedly striding over its moving belt. 'She has as much right to be brought back to the real world as you.'

He went into the control room and studied the monitors. 'Yes. This looks like a good time to do it.' One of the screens showed Lucie trudging down the lane leading to the caravan, loaded with towels and a fold-up chair. He clicked on the *Release* icon. Returning to the other room, he called, 'OK, Lucie. You're back.'

She lifted the headset. 'Phew! That was hard work. You might have brought me back sooner instead of waiting until I'd nearly got all the way back. Oh there you are,' she said, spotting Scott still sitting on the floor. 'What happened to you? The last I saw you were disappearing over the top of the rocks. Did that guy catch up with you?'

Scott described what had happened. Theo

explained for Lucie's benefit what he and Scott had been talking about.

'So, let me get this straight,' Theo resumed, turning back to the boy. 'From now on we stick to Virtutopias where nature is run according to a fixed, dependable, set of laws. Nobody monkeys about with them. Everything reliable and predictable so you can plan ahead sensibly – a neutral environment that treats everyone the same at all times. Is that it?'

Scott thought for a moment, then grudgingly muttered, 'I suppose so.'

'Good. Seriously, I think it's for the best. It all gets a bit too chaotic otherwise. Mind you, there's a price to be paid for consistency. With the laws being fixed and unchanging, there are bound to be times when you'll run foul of them – the laws doing their normal thing; they'll produce some outcome you don't like: earthquakes; tornadoes – that sort of thing. I'll not be able to step in and tweak things. Once I've set it all up, I have to be somewhat hands-off. I have to let the world – and you – be yourselves.'

'Normally, yes,' agreed Lucie. 'I can see that. But that doesn't mean you couldn't intervene *some*times. Not *all* the time. But occasionally – when someone's in real trouble. You could do that. After all, you are in charge of Virtutopia; what you say goes.'

'Oh yes, I *could* intervene. But why would I want to?'

107

'Why? Well . . . Because it would be the decent thing to do; that's why,' she exclaimed indignantly. 'Don't you *care* for the people in Virtutopia?'

'Of course I do.'

'Well, there you are, then. You step in and help people in trouble – in *real* trouble. Not if people ask you for the sun to shine; that was a bit silly, I suppose. But if people are ill or about to die. Why not?'

Theo smiled. 'I'll bear it in mind.'

'That's no answer. Will you, or will you not, intervene when asked? Yes or no?' she insisted.

'I have told you,' replied Theo equally insistently. 'I shall bear such requests in mind. Now come on. Let's get you out of those suits.'

When the children were back in their normal clothes, Scott had a sudden thought. 'Error 137. What is that?' he asked.

'Ah,' said Theo. 'The dreaded 137. Yes, I should have warned you about that. You see with all Virtutopias I have to be careful not to create conditions where it would be impossible for life to exist – obviously – or you wouldn't be there. We can't have you walking around in a world where it would be possible for someone to work out that human beings like yourself could not possibly exist.'

'I don't understand,' said the boy.

'Well, take, for example, that request you put in for water not to be wet. Life is heavily dependent on water. Your own body is – what? Ninety per cent water – something like that? When scientists try to find out whether there might be life on some distant planet, one of the first questions they ask is whether there are any signs of water there. Water is very special to life – meaning, water the way it actually *is* – with all the properties it has. A different kind of "water" – with different properties – that wouldn't work. So when you said 'Make water less wet' that was a recipe for disaster. The program would not allow it. You might have had dry feet, but you'd also have snuffed it. You simply can't mess about with the properties of water.'

'OK. But what about that second message I got – the other 137 – when I was falling. All I asked for was gravity to be made less strong – so I would float down. Where's the harm in that?'

Theo shook his head. 'It's not that simple. Take the way the world began – with a Big Bang. All that came out were gases. These gases had to collect together – under the influence of the gravity forces between the gas particles. The gases squashed down to become stars – like our own star: the sun. Without the warmth of the sun, there could be no life on Earth. If you had a world where gravity was only one tenth what it actually is, the sun would never have formed in the first place – and that would mean no life on Earth.'

He went over to a bookshelf and brought back a thick folder marked *Error 137*.

'If you have time, you might like to thumb through that. It lists the different conditions which *all* versions of Virtutopia *must* satisfy. If any one of them were not satisfied, there could be no life.'

'But there are so many of them,' remarked Scott in surprise, as he scanned the contents.

'Oh yes. Life is a very delicate thing. Conditions have to be just right for it to develop and flourish. That's why the Error 137 overrule function has been built in. It works a bit like an anti-virus check. Any proposed modifications to Virtutopia are automatically checked out by the program to ensure that they won't screw things up. Only if they pass these rigid criteria are they allowed.'

'I had no idea it was such a tricky business designing a Virtutopia,' observed Lucie thoughtfully.

'Or a real world,' Theo added.

'What do you mean?' she asked.

'Well, what we've been saying doesn't just apply to virtual realities, it applies to the world we live in,' he said, gesturing around them. 'This real world had to satisfy all these same criteria too – otherwise we would not be here asking these questions.'

'But I don't understand,' she said with a frown. 'Virtutopia is a home for life because that is the way you designed it. But how did the real world manage to do it?'

'How indeed? That's a question a lot of people are asking. But,' he said, looking up at the clock, 'that's enough of that. Your parents will be wondering where you've got to. Come on, get your coats on.'

When they reached the door, he paused. 'By the way, Harsk has been on to me yet again. He says the marketing people are getting jumpy. They want assurances that I shall be able to meet the deadline for the launch. I told him everything was under control. But we only have, at most, a couple of weeks to decide what kind of Virtutopia we want, OK?'

They nodded.

As they walked down the corridor to the main entrance, Lucie observed, 'I was in the canteen the other day and got talking with this man. I didn't get his name – just some man sitting opposite. He asked what I was doing here – me being a child, and how you don't expect children to be working for VirtuCorp. So, I explained what we were doing.' She suddenly looked flustered. 'I hope that was all right, Theo. It's not a secret what we're doing, is it?'

Theo assured her it was OK.

'Well, after I'd finished telling him about our work, he mentioned you, Theo. I didn't really get it, but it sounded as though he thought you had been the original owner of VirtuCorp. That can't be right, can it?'

'Yes, it's true. I used to be the boss,' replied Theo. 'It all began when I was a young researcher. I had plenty of ideas in those days. I started up VirtuCorp

– as a bit of a laugh, I suppose. It began just like a thousand other small start-up companies. But you know how it is in the computer world. You get a lucky break – and make it big.'

'But I don't understand,' continued Lucie. 'Why aren't you still the boss? This man said you suddenly announced one day that you were giving it up.'

'That's right. That's when I handed over to Harsk.'

'But why? The man said everyone thought . . .' She paused, looking embarrassed.

'They thought what?' asked Theo. 'You don't have to worry. I can guess what they thought.'

'Well . . . He said they thought you were mad to do it.'

'Yes, I know that's what they thought. I can't help it if people don't understand me,' he smiled. 'But no matter. I wanted to retain hands-on involvement. Sitting at a desk all day – being grand and important – being the boss – getting knighted – everyone bowing and scraping to me because they know it is in my power to promote them, give them a pay rise, or kick them out of the firm. That's not what appeals to me. So I let Harsk get on with that side of things.'

'This man didn't like Harsk,' said Lucie. 'I could tell. And you know what Scott and I think. Doesn't it ever worry you: the thought that one day Harsk will rule the world.'

'Harsk rule the world? Whatever gave you that idea?' asked Theo.

'But he will. It's obvious,' insisted Lucie. 'My dad read it in the paper. When we first started out on this project – the papers were full of it. Harsk was saying that one day everyone will spend all their time in Virtutopia – every day, all day long. From then on, the world *will* be Virtutopia. That's what he said. And Virtutopia is made and run by VirtuCorp, and Harsk is the boss of VirtuCorp – so Harsk will be in charge of everything.'

'Well . . . In a way . . .' agreed Theo cautiously. 'But he can only make Virtutopia the way the *public* want it, not as he might want to. If he doesn't please the public with what he produces, people won't buy it, and that will be an end of it.'

'Ah, but what if he starts out by making a perfect world, gets everybody into it, but then slowly changes everything to be the way *he* wants it – without anyone noticing. We could all end up like him. Ugh!'

Theo looked thoughtful. 'So, what you're saying is that everything starts out well – it's a genuine utopia to begin with – but then it sort of goes wrong – all thanks to the scheming Lord of this Virtutopian world.' He nodded slowly. 'You might be right at that.'

They emerged from the VirtuCorp building and began walking down the drive to the main gate.

'But there is something you are overlooking,'

continued Theo. 'In a sense, Harsk runs the show. But who is really *responsible* for Virtutopia? If Harsk were to go, there would be no end of others perfectly capable of stepping into his shoes and doing what he does. But if *I*, on the other hand, were to go, who else knows the first thing about how to design and build a Virtutopia? They would be able to *run* one once I had produced it – but not *build* it. So, who's *really* in charge?'

Fifteen

Deaths in the Family

'Why so glum? asked Theo.

'Aunt Kate. She's died,' replied Lucie, taking off her anorak.

'Oh, I'm sorry to hear that.'

'She was only fifty-two'.

'No great age these days. What was wrong with her?' he asked.

'Cancer. There was nothing they could do about it. They couldn't operate. It had spread all over.'

'I take it you were fond of her.'

'Yes. Very. She had no family of her own, so she used to come and spend Christmas with us. We always looked forward to her coming. She was lots of fun.'

'She visited you that Christmas in Virtutopia, yes?'

Lucie nodded. 'We're going to miss her terribly.' She fought back her tears.

Scott joined them in the control room. 'I can't stand the thought of death,' he said with a shiver.

'That's only natural,' said Theo. 'Most young people worry about death – especially the possibility of your parents dying early – leaving you with no one to look after you.'

Scott nodded. 'And that's not all,' he added. 'Tweet has died too. It happened last night.'

'Tweet? Who is Tweet?' asked Theo puzzled.

'Our canary,' explained Lucie. 'Scott is more upset over Tweet than he is about Aunt Kate.'

'I am not!' declared Scott indignantly. 'I just happen to be an animal lover . . .'

'So? Are you saying I'm not? Just because *I* didn't burst into tears when Dad took the cover off her.'

'I never did,' stormed Scott.

'All right. All right. That's quite enough of that,' interrupted Theo. 'Change the subject. When's the funeral? Your *aunt's* funeral – not the budgie's.'

'Canary's,' corrected Scott.

'Next Tuesday,' replied Lucie.

'You'll be going?'

Again Lucie nodded.

'So you won't be coming here for a session that day,' Theo frowned. 'In that case, we'd better crack on now – that's if you feel up to it, of course,' he added hastily.

The children assured him they were fine.

'So,' said Theo, sitting back and surveying the controls. 'Had any further ideas?'

'Certainly,' announced Lucie. 'A world where there is no death.'

'No *death*?' exclaimed Theo. 'Nobody dies. *Ever*?'

'That's right,' she replied. 'And that goes for animals too.'

'Well, I don't know,' said Theo doubtfully. 'Are

116

you sure you know what you're doing?'

'Of course,' said Scott, warmly. 'Sounds a great idea. How soon can you set it up?'

'Well . . . It wouldn't take long. Half an hour, perhaps. But . . .'

'Fine. Let's get on with it then,' said Scott, going next door to put on his suit.

Theo shrugged. His fingers flew expertly over the keyboard as he re-set the program. After a while, the children, now dressed in their suits and carrying their headsets, joined him and watched as he put the finishing touches to what he was doing.

'Nearly there,' Theo announced. 'Yes . . . That should do it. Execute program . . .'

The screen on the console went blank, there was a bleep, and a message came up: *Error 137*.'

'Oh no,' declared Theo. 'What's gone wrong now?' He leant forward with a puzzled frown.

'Why is it showing that?' asked Lucie. 'I thought Error 137 was all about us trying to do something that would make life impossible. That's what you said. But we're not doing that. We're doing the opposite; we're getting rid of death – so that must be *good* for life. I don't understand.'

'Neither do I,' said Theo. He got up and went over to the bookshelf on the wall. 'Things must be more complicated than we thought.' He took down the folder entitled *Error 137*, returned to his seat, and spent the next few minutes studying it.

Lucie glared at the message on the screen. She muttered impatiently, 'It's *stupid*!'

'No,' murmured Theo. 'Whatever the system is, it is not stupid. And . . . yes . . . I think I see what the trouble is. Yes, that must be it . . .'

'What?' asked Lucie anxiously. 'Is it serious?'

'Oh it's serious all right. It's pointing out that without death there would have been no evolution. Human beings would never have evolved – and so you couldn't exist.'

He closed the folder. Scott and Lucie looked confused. They hadn't a clue what he was on about.

'Evolution. I take it you've done that at school?' asked Theo.

Lucie shrugged uncertainly.

'Hmmm . . .' said Theo thoughtfully rubbing his chin. 'Well, it's a bit like this: take cheetahs. Cheetahs have to chase after antelopes and catch them if they are to have a meal and not starve to death, right? Suppose there are two cheetahs. One is a faster runner than the other. Which one is the more likely to get the meal?'

'The faster one,' replied Scott. 'That's obvious.'

'Right. So the faster cheetah has a better chance of not starving to death. It's going to survive to an age where it can mate and have young. And those young are going to inherit their parent's fast-running ability. The slower-running cheetah, on the other hand, starves to death before it can mate, so it doesn't get a chance to pass on its slow-running characteristic. The result is that the new generation of cheetahs will, on average, be somewhat faster runners than the previous one. And then the generation of cheetahs after that will be even faster runners. The fast-running ability gets selected out.

'And what goes for fast running also goes for any other characteristic that gives its owner an advantage when it comes to finding scarce food or shelter: sharp teeth, sharp claws, a tough protective hide – or in the case of humans, a greater intelligence. This is called 'natural selection'. But for evolution to take place like this, those not lucky enough to have these advantages have to be weeded out – they have to *die*. And I mean they have to die *early* – before they can pass on their not-so-good characteristics. See what I'm getting at?'

Without waiting for a reply, he continued. 'What I'm saying is that without death, life would never have evolved from the simple forms of the past – to complicated creatures like you and me. That's what that Error 137 code is telling us. Anybody living in the kind of Virtutopia I was trying to set up would be able to work out that the theory of evolution was a non-starter. And so they, and you, and animals couldn't exist.'

'Oh,' said Lucie in disappointment. They lapsed into silence.

But then she brightened up. 'But surely,' she continued, 'the whole point of Error 137 is that it is meant to stop people in Virtutopia from finding out that they are living in an unreal world – a world where it could be proved that humans couldn't possibly exist. But all *this* is doing is getting rid of the idea that we came about because of evolution. It wouldn't stop people thinking that humans might have been made some other way.'

'Adam and Eve,' suggested Scott.

'Exactly!' exclaimed Lucie. 'People in the past were perfectly happy to believe they descended from Adam and Eve. Just because they didn't know about evolution, they didn't go around saying "We can't exist. This world cannot be real."'

Theo was still not happy. 'I know that. But today we *do* know we are here because of evolution; we recognise that the early parts of the Bible were never meant to be read that way,' he protested.

'*You* know that,' said Lucie. 'But people in Virtutopia don't have to know it. So there's nothing to stop us going ahead. Right?'

Theo thought long and hard. Then, grudgingly, admitted, 'I guess you're right. It wouldn't *have* to destroy the illusion of reality.'

'Great! Is there a way of getting round *that*?' Lucie asked, pointing to the message on the screen.

'That? Oh that's no problem. It's just a warning to me. I can always override it.'

'So that's it then,' declared Lucie firmly. 'Override the warning – and let's kill off death, once and for all. Come on, Scott,' she called out as she hurried into the other room to mount her platform.

Sixteen

On and On

Mr Harris got home from work, dumped his briefcase on the floor of the hall – instead of taking it upstairs to his study as he normally did – and threw his raincoat over the banister – instead of hanging it up in the hall closet. He was clearly upset about something.

As he entered the sitting room, his wife looked up expectantly from reading the newspaper. He sadly shook his head.

'I'm so sorry, dear,' Mrs Harris said sympathetically. 'Not to worry. These things take time.'

Mr Harris slumped down in an armchair.

'What's the matter?' enquired Lucie who was squatting in front of the TV set.

'Don't bother your father now,' said her mother. 'You can come and help me lay the table for dinner.'

'But all I asked was . . .'

'Lucie!' her mother hissed. 'You heard what I said.'

Lucie reluctantly got up and followed her.

Closing the kitchen door behind them, her mother whispered, 'Sorry about that. But your father has had something of a disappointment. It's best not to trouble him just now.'

'What kind of disappointment?'

'Well, a week ago one of his colleagues at work, Mr Jones, retired – at long last. He was your father's immediate boss. It's the first time in about fifty years anyone has retired from the firm. Naturally enough, your father thought he might have a chance of getting his job – getting promotion.' She shrugged. 'But, apparently, he didn't.'

'Was he *expected* to get it?' asked Lucie, getting the knives and forks out of the drawer.

'Not really. No, not really, I suppose. But he couldn't help setting his heart on it. No, the job probably went to Jack Elliot – another man in the office. Which is only fair. He must be thirty years older than your father. You see, Dad hasn't been with the firm all that long . . . seventy years or so. That's not too long to wait before you get your foot off the bottom rung of the ladder. Jake next door was telling me he's coming up to his hundredth anniversary at Smith's – and he's been doing the same job there all that time.'

Scott entered the kitchen through the back door where he had been emptying the swing-top waste bin.

'Remember to put a plastic liner bag in that,' said his mother.

Scott rolled his eyes upwards. 'How many millions of times have you told me that?'

'Several probably. But you still forget,' replied

his mother. 'Anyway, what did you two learn at school today?'

Scott sighed. 'And how many more times do *we* have to tell *you* we don't learn things at school – not any more. It must be thirty years since I last learned something at school. There's nothing more to learn.'

'So you keep saying. What I don't understand is what you do with your time there if you don't learn things,' commented his mother as she began dishing out the food.

'We hang about. We wait. We wait for the Employment Agency to ring up the school to say there is a job vacancy. There hasn't been one this year – or last year. So we wait. And that's all there is to it. It's boring.'

'We must all learn a little patience,' chided Mrs Harris.

'Here we go again: Patience is a Virtue,' said Scott in a mocking sing-song tone of voice.

His mother ignored him. 'Lucie, go tell your father dinner's ready, please.'

When they had finished the meal, the children cleared the table. Mrs Harris made coffee for herself and her husband, and they all settled down in the lounge. Mr Harris switched the TV on. It was the early evening news.

'That's a point,' remarked Scott. 'Why do they call it "news"? There's never anything "new" about it. It's always the same old stuff.'

'Today's news *is* important,' said his father. 'It's Budget Day.'

'So what?' Scott replied. Standing up, and making as if he were clutching the lapels of his non-existent jacket, he solemnly declared, 'Budget Day. I regret to announce that I am as of today having to put up the taxes . . . Shock! Horror! . . .'

'Shut up, will you,' demanded Mr Harris angrily. 'I can't hear.'

The news announcer was saying: 'The Chancellor of the Exchequer, in his statement to the House this afternoon declared that the demands on the National Health Service had soared in the past year due once again to the escalating costs of caring for the elderly. Extra funds of thirty billion pounds were to be found from two sources: An increase in the basic rate of income tax from sixty-five percent to sixty-seven per cent . . .'

'What was I telling you . . .' murmured Scott under his breath – only to be silenced by a disapproving look from his mother.

' . . . and an increase in the age at which one becomes eligible for a pension from 270 to 290 years,' continued the newsreader. 'At this, the leader of the Opposition sprang to his feet to protest. He called the increase in the retirement age "scandalous". He went on to ask, "Was the Chancellor aware that almost a third of the present work force is crippled with arthritis and can only get to work with special transport, and ten per cent of the work force are officially suffering from the early stages of Alzheimer's disease. The proposed raising yet further of the retirement age would mean an even higher proportion of the work force will not actually be fit for work. Had the Chancellor taken into account the hidden costs of what this would mean in terms of lost days from work because of sickness, and the provision of extra facilities at work for the disabled?"

'The Chancellor replied that the move was regrettable but inevitable. As we all know, the vast majority of the population is elderly. Currently each active worker has to support 4.2 elderly people of pensionable age. It is difficult to see how this ratio can be allowed to worsen.

'The Health Minister welcomed the statement even though the new funds to the NHS fell far short of what was required. With seventy per cent of retirees now incapable of looking after themselves because of mental and physical ill-health, the needs of the NHS were first priority . . .'

'Can we . . .' began Mrs Harris tentatively. 'Can we switch it off now, dear. I think we have had enough depressing news for one day.'

'Yes, I suppose so,' agreed Mr Harris. 'Sorry to be so ratty. It's been one of those days.'

'We know, dear,' said his wife understandingly.

With the TV off, they each settled down to reading. It wasn't long before Lucie murmured, 'How stupid. Where else are they going to walk?'

'What's that, dear?' asked her mother.

'It says here "They went for a walk in the country." Well, I ask you. If you're in Britain, where else are you going to walk except in Britain – you're bound to be walking in the country.'

Mrs Harris laughed. 'No, no. It's not that sort of "country". They don't mean Britain or France. They mean "country" as in "countryside".'

'Countryside? What's that?' asked Scott.

'Oh that's going back a long time,' intervened Mr Harris. 'In the olden days there used to be fields and trees . . .'

'Fields of grass, do you mean?' asked Lucie.

'That's right. Big open spaces.'

'How big? As big as our garden patio?'

'No, no. Much bigger. The countryside would go on for miles.'

'*Miles*! Just fields?' exclaimed Scott.

'Fields, trees, bushes, hedges.'

'No houses?'

'The occasional farmhouse possibly, but often not even that.'

'What a waste of space!' exclaimed Scott.

'I wouldn't call it that,' said his mother. 'I think it must have been rather nice walking in fields of grass and being surrounded by trees.'

'So, what happened to it all?' asked Lucie, getting interested.

'It got built on – until there was none left. They had to. The population just keeps going up and up.'

'How did people manage not to have such big populations back then?'

'They died. They lived seventy to eighty or so years and died.'

'Seventy to eighty years! Is that all? They all died as children?'

'Not exactly children. They aged much quicker in those days. You'd be an adult by the time you were in your twenties.'

'*What*!' exclaimed Scott disbelievingly. 'People left school at twenty – and got jobs?'

'Even before they were twenty. Yes, in those days people died – they got out of the way, and made room for other people,' he added with a rueful smile.

'How sensible,' observed Lucie. 'That's a really good idea.'

'Well, I don't know about that,' said her father. 'But certainly in those days you didn't have to hang around long to get your hard-earned promotion.'

'I agree with you, Mum. I reckon I would have liked going for a walk in the country,' said Lucie thoughtfully.

'So, is it time to go to bed yet?' interrupted Scott.

His mother looked at the clock. 'Not yet. Another couple of hours to go.'

'But there's nothing to do. I am *so* bored. Being asleep is the best part of the day; it makes the time go faster.'

'For goodness' sake, read a book – like your sister,' suggested his mother.

'I've read them. All of them. Lots of times. Do you want me to recite one to you?'

'No, thank you. You can have a go at a jigsaw instead.'

'I've done them all – millions of times.'

'You could give your room a good tidy.'

'Some day. There's no need to do it now. Perhaps tomorrow, or the next day, or next week, or next year. There's plenty of time to do that sort of thing.'

Lucie looked up. 'It's funny that, don't you think. When you have all the time in the world you never seem to get around to doing anything. How on earth did they manage when they lived for only seventy years?'

'I sometimes wonder that myself,' said her mother with a far-away look in her eye. 'I suppose they just got on with things. There was a sense of urgency.'

'Urgency? What's "urgency"? What does that mean?' asked Scott.

'Oh it's a word people used to use – when they did not have much time.'

They drifted into silence – a long silence – interrupted eventually by Scott, 'I'm bored. *So* bored.'

'I know, dear,' said his mother. 'But that's life, isn't it.'

Seventeen

Moderation in all Things

As Lucie and Scott entered the VirtuCorp building they were surprised to find Theo waiting for them by the reception desk in the entrance hall.

'Hi, Theo,' said Scott. 'What are you doing here? We know our way up to the lab.'

'We're not going to the lab – not today,' Theo replied. 'We're out of time. They've called a board meeting for the end of the week. I have to let Harsk have our final report by tomorrow morning so it can be circulated to the directors.'

He led them to the Visitors' Lounge, and signalled

for them to sit on a sofa as he settled down in an armchair opposite. He opened his briefcase and pulled out a pad of notepaper. With pen poised he announced, 'We've simply got to make up our minds. We have to decide what kind of Virtutopia we are recommending. So, where shall we begin? I take it you want there to be no death.'

As he began writing, Scott looked searchingly at Lucie. 'Er . . . I'm not sure.'

'No,' agreed Lucie. 'We're not sure. You see, we had a discussion yesterday – when we got home after the session – Scott and me. Frankly, we don't know what to think. That business yesterday about death was just about the last straw. We had thought that with death there would be no problem. It was obviously a bad thing – so get rid of it. But now . . . after yesterday . . . we don't know. It didn't turn out the way we thought.'

Theo crossed out what he had written. 'So, we keep death. What about having everything you want . . . what about winning all the time . . . . 275 calls . . .?'

The children shook their heads. 'We've been through all that,' said Lucie.

'Nothing we've tried worked out – not the way we thought it would,' said Scott sadly. 'I don't know. It just sort of turned out differently.'

Theo nodded. 'That's what I suspected all along. I thought that might be the way it went. That's why I got you to try out the ideas before we went ahead and built them into Virtutopia.'

'Mind you, we did have a new idea, didn't we, Scott?' Lucie said more hopefully.

'We did?' Scott frowned, thought for a moment, and then brightened up. 'Oh yes, *that*. Yes. You tell him about that.'

'Yes. You see, Theo, we reckoned that perhaps the problem – with all the Virtutopias we have tried out – is that we've been overdoing things – making the changes too drastic.'

'Meaning?' asked Theo.

'What she means,' said Scott cutting in, 'is that we started out with everyone having *everything* they wanted – absolutely everything. *That* was the mistake. What we should have done is not ask for *everything*, but just *more* of what we want – a lot more – but not everything. Not too much.' He regarded Theo expectantly. 'What do you think about that? That way we would still have things to look forward to. People could still buy things for others at Christmas – things they hadn't already got. We think that would work. Yes?'

Theo looked doubtful. 'What exactly do you mean by "not too much"?'

Scott shrugged. 'You know. A lot – but not too much.'

Theo shook his head. 'No. I don't know.'

'Now you're just being awkward,' declared Scott crossly.

'Put it like this,' replied Theo. 'As far as I am concerned, you kids these days have unbelievably more than I had as a kid . . .'

The children looked at each other as if to say, 'Here we go. Typical grown-up lecture coming.'

'Pull those faces if you like,' he continued. 'It doesn't alter the fact that it is true – any more than it alters the fact that you don't seem to be any the happier for it. None of you is satisfied. Does it never occur to you that you might have too much *already*?'

'Well, forget about us having things,' said Lucie changing tack. 'What about evil? We wanted a world without evil – no evil *at all*. What we didn't realise is that that would make us no better than robots. But what if . . . Yes, what if we had gone for something less than a total ban on evil. Suppose we did not get rid of it altogether – just got rid of the worst of it – leaving people to be . . . well, a little bit bad – if that's what they want – but not totally evil.'

'Yeah. That's good,' said Scott, warming to the idea. 'And we could do the same with pain. We could cut down on the pain so it was never really bad – never agonising – but just enough to give us a gentle warning when things were going wrong – when we get burned or have something go wrong with the appendix.'

'Yes, and when things go wrong – really badly wrong,' continued his sister, 'then you would step in and intervene and help out. We wouldn't call on you all the time – like we did when we wanted the sun to shine at the beach or when we wanted the bus to come quickly. We'd just use the 275 call in emergencies – real emergencies.'

There was a long pause, before Theo replied quietly, 'Tell me, do you know of any people who already live this kind of life – someone who has things nice and easy, lots of money, though not exactly a billionaire; someone who has never really been ill or had a lot of pain, someone who's been molly-coddled?'

'Dorothea Cholmondley!' The children declared in unison, bursting into laughter.

Theo looked puzzled. 'Would someone kindly . . .? Dorothea who . . .?'

They explained how they had once met this frightfully spoilt upper-class girl staying at the same hotel when on holiday – though this Dorothea and her family were staying in the fabulously expensive penthouse suite.

'Stuck-up pig!' exclaimed Scott.

'Really, Scott,' said Lucie with a look of disdain. 'Well-brought-up people do not speak like that. You are so-o, so-o unkind. You should know better,' she said in her poshest accent – before collapsing in giggles.

'You're quite right. It's unkind,' replied Scott, 'but ever so *true*.'

Theo waited patiently. Eventually the laughter subsided and Lucie was able to continue. 'Sorry, Theo,' she said as she collected herself. 'Dorothea went to this posh school. Her parents didn't want her to be contaminated by having to mix with the riff-raff at the local comprehensive – *our* sort, she meant. The worst thing that ever happened to her in her whole life was the day she was trying to put up the deckchair on the beach . . .'

' . . . and she broke her nail,' added Scott. 'Her little, teeny-weeny finger nail.' This was the signal for yet more laughter.

'Sorry. But I don't see what's so funny,' said Theo clearly beginning to get annoyed.

'Oh it was nothing really, I suppose,' said Lucie. 'You had to be there – to see how she reacted. She howled and howled. You'd have thought it was a total disaster.'

'But it was a disaster – for *her*,' said Theo solemnly. 'For her that is exactly what it was. A total disaster. It might have been the very worst thing that had ever happened to her. She had no other bad experiences to compare it with. You really mustn't be too hard on her. Cast your own minds back – to the first time you fell down and banged your head. You probably can't remember it now. But I bet you cried – I bet you howled your eyes out. It seemed dreadful at the time – a disaster. Nowadays you take such knocks in your stride – part and parcel of everyday living. You've suffered far worse things since. For you, as you are *now*, falling down seems a completely trivial event – not worth thinking about. But not back then when you had nothing else to compare it with.'

'So, what are you saying?' asked Lucie suspiciously. 'Why are we discussing Dorothea at all?'

'What I am saying,' said Theo, 'is that everything is *relative*.'

He sat back in his armchair and gazed intently at them. 'If we were to follow your idea and have a Virtutopia that offered no more than a pampered, frothy existence where you just *play* at life, everything trivialised, no depth – you do a little bit of good and a little bit of bad, you suffer a little, you love a little, you hate a little – everything in small doses . . . All these small doses are going to become magnified in your mind anyway; you can't help it; they will assume a shock-horror significance they don't actually deserve. What kind of life is that? Why bother living such a trivial life *at all*?'

He regarded them sternly.

'Tell me,' he said. 'Who are the finest – and the worst – people you have ever met or heard of? No, don't tell me. *I'll* tell *you*. They are those who have been through the most; those who have suffered the most; those who have pushed themselves to the limit and taken up the severest challenges. In short, those who have lived life *to the full*. So, please, *please* – no half measures, I beg of you. I have not gone to all this time and trouble creating Virtutopia simply to end up creating a Toy World – a world fit for nothing more than a playschool. Virtutopia has to be the *real thing*. So come on. No more talk. You have to *decide*!'

Eighteen

The Decision

'Is this some kind of joke?' barked Lord Harsk looking up from his papers.

It was hard to tell which looked the more severe: the face of the VirtuCorp Chief Executive Officer glowering out of the portrait filling the end wall of the room, or the man himself sitting beneath it.

'*Well*?' he hissed at his Senior Scientist, sitting at the far end. The other members of the Board of Directors, positioned round the sides of the highly polished oval table, shifted uncomfortably. They could tell the signs. The boss was in a filthy mood. They buried their heads in their copies of the report, pretending to study it.

'I'm not sure what you are getting at, sir,' replied Theo innocently. 'I thought the report made things pretty clear. If there is anything . . .'

'It says here the Virtutopia you are proposing should not provide everyone with all they want,' rasped Harsk, spreading his hands out in a gesture of complete disbelief. 'Why ever not? That was to be one of the big selling points.'

'The reason is spelt out in the body of the report. With respect, you may have had time to read only the summary of our findings . . .'

'I have read the whole report,' Harsk interrupted angrily. 'I repeat: why shouldn't everybody have exactly what they want? It doesn't cost us anything; it's all *virtual*.'

'Of course, of course. Cost doesn't come into it. But surely, sir,' Theo said soothingly, 'it is not an altogether surprising conclusion. Rich people aren't known for being happy . . .'

'*I* am perfectly happy, thank you,' Harsk stated – a remark which raised quite a few incredulous eyebrows round the table.

'That's as may be,' continued Theo with a faint smile, 'but you must surely agree that whatever you – or anyone else – has, you soon get used to it – take it for granted. With material goods, the more you get, the more you want; it's a kind of drug. The most it can do for you is give you a temporary lift as you acquire whatever it is. Also, much of the attraction of having things is to go one better than other people . . .'

The Company Secretary, sitting on Harsk's immediate right, shot Theo a warning glance. No one present needed reminding of the ugly scene at the previous meeting when the Board had been bullied by Harsk into giving him an enormous pay rise – for no other reason than that the managing director of a rival firm had recently received a pay rise that had taken his salary above that of Harsk. Theo, however, seemed oblivious to the danger of upsetting Harsk even further – or then again, perhaps he did know, but didn't care.

'As you are aware,' he continued, 'in Virtutopia, everyone has to be treated the same. So, if the rule is that *you* have all you want, then so must everyone else. You cannot be one up on the Joneses,' he added meaningfully, staring straight at Harsk. 'Another point: one of the good things about life is to have things to look forward to. It gives one a sense of purpose and direction. One has the pleasure of anticipation. But if one already has everything, there's nothing to look forward to. Life can become somewhat aimless. It's not for nothing suicide rates are highest in those countries with the highest standards of living.'

'All right, all right,' interrupted Harsk irritably, consulting his notes and turning to another part of the report. 'Let's move on. What's all this about not taking the opportunity to eliminate evil once and for all. That was to be another great attraction. Here, you are proposing to continue to allow people to do whatever *they* decide they want to do.' He looked up in bewilderment. 'I don't believe this. We *know* what people get up to when they are left to their own devices. They make a mess of things – a thorough mess of everything. You'll not get rid of crime that way. You'll still get stealing, armed robberies, muggings. And – heaven forbid – murder.' He gazed round the table. 'Gentlemen, ladies, I ask you. A murder in Virtutopia! When news of that gets out to the media, we're done for. Curtains. Pack your bags; we're all out of a job.'

He thought for a moment, and frowned. 'Come to think of it, we've been through all this before. Those kids of yours – the ones I met in the canteen the other day. They were going on about this kind of nonsense. You remember, Birkin? I discussed it with them. I sorted it all out for them. So why are you still harping on about it?'

'Well,' replied Theo, 'I guess we weren't convinced by your arguments. Again, sir, you have to give yourself a chance to digest the main report. There you will discover the reasons . . .'

'And here on page 26,' said Harsk, ignoring him. 'Pain! You are going to allow people to suffer pain? In Virtutopia!' With that he shut the report with a loud thwack – and violently threw it across the

room. The members instinctively ducked – they were used to his tantrums.

'That's what Lucie and Scott eventually decided,' resumed Theo, quite unconcerned at the scene he had just witnessed.

'Lucie and Scott? Who the hell are they?' Harsk demanded.

'The children – the ones who were testing out . . .' began Theo.

'Oh for God's sake! You're not still going on about *them*. Miserable, ungrateful brats. I thought I told you to get rid of them.'

'Not in so many words . . .'

'Are you saying this report was written by them?'

'Not exactly. I wrote it, but it *was* based on the children's research.'

Harsk roared with derisive laughter. A few of the others also couldn't help smiling. 'Have you taken leave of your senses? *Research*? Pah!'

When calm had been restored once more, the Managing Director ventured, 'Ahem. Can I go back to paragraph 7 of the Summary? Theo, you seem to have abandoned the idea of everyone winning all the time. I would be very sorry to see that go. I personally was looking forward to the time when I was going to win the gold medal in the Virtutopian Olympic marathon run.' Again there was general amusement.

'Yes, I am sure that would have been very rewarding for you,' said Theo. 'One slight problem though: In order for you to enjoy that achievement, who were you going to beat? Who was going to have to lose?'

'Lose? The others of course . . .' replied the Managing Director. But then his face fell. 'Oh, I see what you mean . . .'

'Quite.'

'May I . . .?' murmured the Company Secretary, looking nervously across at Lord Harsk. The boss nodded curtly. 'Thank you, sir. Page 45. No interventions? It says here, "The Operator of Virtutopia will not interfere with what's going on – he cannot be expected to respond to requests for assistance." Isn't that restriction rather unnecessary? Surely he is perfectly capable of interfering – any time he wants.'

'Of course,' said Theo.

'So why not?'

'The children found the 275 option was . . .'

'275?' muttered Harsk. 'What is he rambling on about now?'

The Company Secretary leant across and pointed out to him the relevant section in his copy of the report. Theo went on to explain how the 275 calls led to too many clashes of interest – how it was best to have a neutral environment where everyone knows the rules – and puts up with it. Which wouldn't necessarily rule out the possible occasional intervention by the Operator – if circumstances really merited it.

'Occasional?' asked the Company Secretary. 'How occasional is "occasional"?'

'What I had in mind was *very* occasional,' replied Theo. 'So occasional that most people would doubt that they ever occurred, or even *could* occur.'

'Oh, I say!' exclaimed the Technical Director. 'I'm not having this! Paragraph 14 of the Summary. It says here we are not going to take the opportunity to get rid of death! We are not to be allowed to live for ever. That's a bit much. I object to that. It took me ages sorting out a way round that problem.'

Some of the members looked puzzled. 'Oh come on. You remember,' he went on. 'How can someone who's going to live to seventy or so – in *reality* – how can that same person live *for ever* in Virtutopia? And I came up with the solution: *accelerated time*. All the action in Virtutopia was to be fast-forwarded compared to real time in this world. That way the person in Virtutopia would pack in vastly more virtual experiences than would be possible in a normal lifetime. Virtutopia would give the illusion of life going on for ever. Now, if I am to understand you, you're proposing to ditch the whole thing. It's madness.'

'You will find the children's justification for that beginning on page . . .' Theo thumbed through the report. 'Yes, you'll find that on page 65. If you are not convinced I can ask the children to come in and explain. They are waiting in Reception in case they are required . . .'

'That will not be necessary,' declared Harsk abruptly. 'This is a *board meeting*, not a school classroom. The deliberations of board meetings are strictly confidential. We can't have *anybody* wandering in here off the street – or off the *playground* – and overhearing our decisions.'

'Can I make a suggestion?' an elderly man tentatively offered. 'In the light of what Dr Birkin and his, ahem, assistants have been finding out, perhaps we could compromise. Perhaps we were a little too ambitious in our original conception of Virtutopia: everyone has *everything* they want; there is *no* evil; *no* suffering; *no* death, and so on. How about a little of everything. Everything in moderation?'

Theo was about to explain that he and the children had already been through all that, when the Marketing Director saved him the trouble. 'I'm sorry, Harold, but that's a non-starter. In marketing terms alone, it simply will not work. It's too insipid. If we are to go ahead with Virtutopia, the advertising has to be *strong*. We need good powerful catch phrases. A *perfect* world – a utopian world – that I can sell. Something that's just a slight improvement on the original . . . No. I'm sorry. That just won't run – not at the price we have to charge for the suits, the platforms, etc. etc. The only thing in favour of your suggestion, Harold, is that at least it is an improvement on what Theo is proposing.' He turned to the Senior Scientist.

'Theo, correct me if I am wrong. I have carefully studied your report from cover to cover. It is my assessment that the kind of Virtutopia you have come up with is – quite frankly – *identical to the real world*. Would you say that was a fair summary?'

All eyes turned on Theo. He looked round the table, and then quietly said, 'Yes. I would say that was a fair summary.'

There was a stunned silence. The Marketing Director slowly and deliberately closed his copy of the report. 'Gentlemen, I don't have to emphasise just how serious this is. In a nutshell, I have to ask: why should anyone go to all the expense of buying a cybersuit and paying to log on to IPVR to create virtual experiences when you can have identically the same experiences in the real world for *nothing*. How is Marketing supposed to sell that concept?'

The Financial Director nodded. 'I agree. Allow me, if I may, to recap how we come to find ourselves in this situation. When we first perfected the virtual world of IPVR, sales initially boomed. But then, as you know, the novelty quickly wore off; the bubble burst. People admired the quality of the product we were producing – how real it all seemed – how faithfully it reproduced the conditions of the real world, but so what? Apart from specialist uses – flight simulators for training pilots, and that sort of thing – it did not catch on – not with the public – not the way we had hoped for. As Reg says, why pay for something fake when you can get the real one for nothing. That's why we were running into financial difficulties. But then came the idea of Virtutopia – it was to far exceed anything the real world could offer – it was to be the ultimate perfect world. Now . . .' he spread his hands despairingly. 'Now it would appear that Virtutopia was nothing more than a mirage – and we are facing the abyss once more.'

All eyes turned to Lord Harsk. But if they were expecting him to come up with some solution to their problems, they were to be disappointed. The great Lord Harsk just sat there in a pathetic crumpled heap under the stern, and still confident gaze of his portrait.

Nineteen

Epilogue

It was a beautiful sunny afternoon, but those leaving the Headquarters of VirtuCorp were in sombre mood. There were long and earnest farewells, much shaking of hands, appeals to stay in touch, and good wishes for the future.

Among the throng was Theo Birkin. After a brief and somewhat rueful look back at the building, he strode down the main driveway towards the entrance gate. There, to his surprise, were Lucie and Scott. They were standing next to the security guard, watching workers dismantling the VirtuCorp sign.

'Hullo. What are you two doing here?' asked Theo, clearly pleased to see them.

'Hi,' said Scott. 'We knew it was your last day so we've been waiting – since we came out of school.'

'Fancy an ice-cream, or Pepsi?' asked Theo, nodding in the direction of the coffee bar across the road from the entrance.

'You bet,' they replied, as they fell in step with him.

Having got their orders at the counter, they settled down at a table in the window looking across at the VirtuCorp building.

'Well. I must say, it was very nice of you to come,' said Theo.

'We could hardly let you go without saying how sorry we are,' murmured Lucie apologetically.

'Sorry? What about?'

'Well . . . You getting the sack and all that.'

'I am being made redundant – that's what it's called. It's more polite if you put it like that,' said Theo with an amused expression. 'Besides it's not just me. We are all in the same boat,' he continued, looking across the road at the stream of employees – or *ex*-employees – pouring out of the gates. 'VirtuCorp has gone bust; it's finished.'

'That makes us feel even worse,' replied Lucie.

'But why? What has any of this got to do with you?'

'Because it's all our fault – that's why,' said Scott. 'That's what you said – after that meeting last

149

month – the one where you presented them with our report.'

'I said nothing of the kind!' exclaimed Theo with a worried frown. 'Whatever gave you that idea? I wasn't blaming *you*. You must have got hold of the wrong end of the stick. I'm sorry. Perhaps I didn't express myself clearly . . . I never intended . . .'

Theo was clearly upset. 'Look . . . It was going to happen anyway. The whole idea of Virtutopia . . . Well, it was never going to work out. That's what I always suspected – right from the very beginning – before you even joined the project. You must have known – or at least suspected – I was sceptical about the whole thing. It was only a matter of time before Virtutopia was exposed as the fraud it is. And it is far better for it to come out into the open *now* rather than later. That way fewer people get hurt – all those people who were set to spend a small fortune on cybersuits – only to be disappointed when it did not bring the expected results. No, the world is in your debt.'

'But I don't understand why the company went bust,' Lucie frowned. 'OK, so Virtutopia turned out to be a bad idea, but what about the normal IPVR? They could still have carried on with that – making a virtual world that was just like the real one. That was really clever.'

'Clever, yes. But cleverness itself is never enough. It was well done – very realistic. But there was no profit in it. The novelty was already wearing off before the Virtutopia project was launched. Sales of the cybersuits were steadily declining – they were too expensive for what they were able to deliver. And that's why the company gambled on the idea of creating the perfect world. *That* was something they *would* be able to sell – so they thought.'

'I feel sorry for the employees,' said Lucie.

'Yes, it's an upsetting time for them. But not to worry. They'll get other jobs before long. They're first-rate people; they will be in demand. When I first set up VirtuCorp, I made a point of taking on only the very best and brightest people. There's always a demand for that sort. Not for Lord Harsk,' he added with a wry smile. 'That's another matter altogether. He is the one who will suffer.'

'Why?' asked Scott.

'He went ahead too fast. He ordered the manufacture of vast quantities of cybersuits. He anticipated enormous sales as soon as Virtutopia went online. He wanted to be sure they would not run out of supplies. That meant VirtuCorp taking out huge loans to pay for them. They ended up with a mountain of cybersuits, which as soon as the Virtutopia project died, no one wanted any more. The banks immediately called in their loans – which the firm could not pay. And that was the end for VirtuCorp – and for Harsk personally. It is not that anyone *liked* the man anyway. They were prepared to do business with him for as long as he remained successful. But now . . . after a blunder like that . . . no company will touch him with a bargepole. It's tough being the boss,' he added with a twinkle in his eye.

'Yes, but you yourself must be sad. All that wasted effort.'

'Not really. Virtutopia served its purpose.'

'Meaning what?' asked Lucie. 'What purpose?'

'Oh, I don't know. In a funny sort of way, I suppose, it makes us appreciate the world we live in – the *real* world. Anyway. Finished with that drink?'

They got up and Theo paid the bill before leading them out of the coffee shop.

'So what will you be doing with yourself now?' asked Lucie as they began to amble down the street on the way home.

'Me? Oh I shall now have time to concentrate on my main project.'

'*Main* project?' exclaimed Lucie. 'But I thought *that* was your main work,' she said, looking back over her shoulder at the VirtuCorp building.

'IPVR? Virtutopia?' said Theo raising his eyebrows and shaking his head. 'Oh, dear me, no. That was never more than a sideline. No. I'm moving on.'

'So?' said Scott taking an interest. 'Go on. Tell us. What is your *main* project?'

Theo did not answer straight away. Eventually he replied, cautiously, 'I am mainly concerned with another type of world.'

152

'Another one?' exclaimed Scott all agog. 'Another VR?'

'Some might call it virtual – meaning 'not real' – but that is not how *I* see it.'

'So,' joined in Lucie. 'Tell us about it. What is it like?'

'There's not much I can say . . .'

'Why not? Is it a deadly secret?'

'No, no. It's just that it's hard to put into words. It is an existence that cannot be explained and described in ordinary language. Ordinary language was devised to talk about *this* world,' he said indicating the trees and houses they were passing. 'This *kind* of reality – or imagined variations of this kind of world. But ordinary language isn't matched to this other type of reality. It is quite powerless to describe it. No, people simply have to experience it. Once they have experienced it, and met up with other people who have experienced it too, then they might start to develop a language – a way of talking – that models their experiences and can describe that world, but not before.'

'Is it a good world to be in?' asked Scott eagerly. 'As good as Virtutopia – or as good as we once *thought* Virtutopia might be?'

'Better.'

'Better!' cried Scott.

'Oh yes,' replied Theo with a faraway look in his eye. 'Much, much better than you or anyone can ever dream of.'

'A *perfect* world?' ventured Lucie.

'Yes, you could call it that.'

'But I don't understand. How have you got round the problems we had with designing Virtutopia?'

'Ah,' replied Theo mysteriously. 'You'll have to be patient. One day you'll find out – assuming you are one of the chosen,' he added.

'Hey, I can't wait to have a go,' said Scott urgently. 'When can we try it?'

'Hold on, hold on,' frowned Theo. 'Who said you were going to have a go?'

'Well, after the good job we did with our other project,' said Scott indignantly, 'I'd have thought we had earned the right . . .'

'No one *earns* the right to enter this other world of mine,' declared Theo sternly.

'OK. How much does it cost? How long do I have to save up?'

'No one *buys* their way in either. In fact, rich people find it especially difficult to qualify.'

'Qualify?' said Lucie, joining in. 'Are you saying you have to *qualify*? So not everyone is allowed in your other world?'

'*Everyone*? Goodness me, no. Very few people find the way in.'

'You have to sit a really tough exam to qualify. Is that it? You have to be clever – a genius?' continued Lucie.

'Not at all,' was the reply. 'But you do have to have special qualities.'

'Such as?' asked Scott.

'I get it,' butted in Lucie. 'It's meant to be a perfect world, so you only allow in people who have already shown that they are perfect.'

Scott's face dropped. 'I knew there must be some catch. This world of yours is only for goody-goody types of people.'

Theo laughed out loud. 'Oh dear me, no. I wouldn't call it that. It'll be home to quite a few rogues, I can tell you. No, you don't have to be perfect. But you do have to have the right attitude. You do have to be able to demonstrate that your heart is in the right place.'

They reached the crossroads. The sun had set by now and the street lamps were coming on.

'But enough of that,' announced Theo. 'This is where we part company.'

'For good?' the children asked sadly.

'Bless you, no. I simply meant I have to turn down here; you go straight on, right? You know where I live. I'm always ready for a chat. Just give me a call.'

'275?' asked Scott with a grin.

Theo winked. 'The number in the directory is probably more reliable.'